MOAV

by

THE RATHS

The future is nothing at all, unless...

THE RATHS

CONTENTS

ACKNOWLEDGMENTS

There is nothing to acknowledge.

CHAPTER ONE

The North sea and the slowly eroding cliffs of Dunbar continue their magnetic dialogue as black waves surge to shore. A short walk from the rocky lip of the promontory, to the civilizing vista of close-cropped grass where bottle green blades stand to attention under a slate grey sky.

Tumultuous clouds. A nuclear power station opened by the Iron Lady threatening in the distance, beneath its atom-hot giant feet swarms of jellyfish bathe in the unnatural warmth. The station is old, extended many times past its use-by dates by its eager off- shore owners. Jobs! Jobs! The locals tolerate the jellyfish, but dogs can no longer swim in the water. The land is still something of a magnificent miracle, if you blot out the radioactive time bomb and cement works billowing snakes of black smoke. These minor inconveniences and major necessities are deleted from memory, and it is the famous Greens that consecrate the area's living standards and ensure houses unaffordable to any but the supremely endowed few.

The geometric deliberations of a golf course, manicured by laymen, coveted by fanatics. These be-holed crop circles surround a clubhouse made of stone and slate, faithful to the fashion of thousands of dwellings embossing the Scottish mainland. And at this mecca, a small boy plays in a courtyard.

Six year old Arthur drags a stick, swirling patterns in the gravel, waiting for his grandfather. He has a soft face and large blue eyes, tufts of gingery blonde hair stick out unevenly on his head. He traces patterns to replicate a tessellation of ideas in his imagination, secret labyrinths and daring escape routes.

The old threat. Two boys, Jayden and Matt, play by the door of the clubhouse trading sports cards: yells and skirmishes indicate a fraught negotiation.

As Arthur's solitary stick separates the rough grey stones, something small tries to traverse the Pyreneen landscape: a bumble bee. The boy crouches down to see it up close: the yellow and brown furry body, its agonisingly slow pace. Trying to crawl.

The creature is dying. It's miniscule movement a Herculean labour. Luminous blue eyes dilate in the observation of these small endeavours, these huge trials. After a moment of watching, Arthur's mouth and jaw become tense. He stiffens in the wind, bracing as it lashes his hair onto his cheeks. God is in the detail. But whether God is in the Clouds, in the centre of the earth, or in Arthur's limitless imagination, God is somewhere other. Abandonment of self to the infallible dimension. And in that moment of abandon, total vulnerability, when out on a golf course on a rainy Saturday when Grandfather works his third shift in a week despite having retired and getting a measly pension which doesn't stretch to cover groceries even when shopping at Asda and the Boys playing cards and learning how to be Men are a clear and present danger to an orange haired boy seeing his first up close witnessing of a raspberry-gorging Bombus Pascuorum Queen, fur still branched to gather pollen, to feed the hive and in turn feed the world.

Arthur stands erect. Expressionless.

In the distance, thunder rumbles like a slow rebuke. Arthur casts his eyes to the sky, pupils reflecting the oncoming storm. Furtive movements, a crouch, a snap of the head, flash of the eyes, the working of fingers. The hasty construction of a fortress, gravel as bricks and mortar, stones as pillars.

Inside, the Dying Bee: Sovereign of the Grey Walls.

An old man, skin lined across broad cheekbones and fading jaw, hair the colour of wheat left out past the harvest. Navy eyes and even features, a strong voice bellowing a command: "Arthur!"

I bid adieu and blessed be to the Sovereign of the Grey Walls.

Arthur runs, skirting past the vendors of cards and paraphernalia and juvenilia to the cold kitchen where Grandfather is waiting.

3

He hears the boys snigger and alliterate his name, but he remembers King Arthur and rises above over the whip of humiliation by summoning a compassion for the boys who spend their Saturdays playing futile games which stoke a fire for endless consumerism and mental passivity instead of dreaming of labyrinths and monsters and famous WW2 escape routes. He considers these to be benevolent thoughts, especially for his age. But thoughts of benevolence turn to the bee, and the compassion that provided a salve to the stinging barbs has in turn churned to a fear that sits like sick in his stomach for the loneliness of that unwell sovereign, dying far from her aerial home.

Jayden and Matt despise the ginger with almost exactly the same ardour by which they unwittingly need him. He is easy meat, and the markets are often empty. Consider the pent up agitation, the need to strut and bellow, deprived of the nearest way. Lightning rods of easily forgotten aggressions unable to earth, zigzagging around the skies like the bolts of a demented Zeus.

Arthur scurries by, a weakling. A loser. They try out a few new jeers, then laugh it off. Oh invigorating release. Jayden organizes his cards, ready for the next hustle, while Matt looks in the distance from where Arthur came. The blood instinct of a destroyer, sensing an unexplored horizon.

Matt walks toward Arthur's gravel markings. The stick is lying on the ground, surely begging to be picked up and brandished like a sword. As he spins into the centre of the courtyard, he spies a little mound of rocks. Curiously close to the strange ginger haired cry-baby and the scene of his bizarre galumphing. The stick falls to Matt's side as the castle roof is lifted.

"We got a live one!"

Disputable by anyone's reckoning, but the promise of answering the call with death sees Jayden sprint over. They circle the bee. It is barely moving, save an occasional attempt to lift a leg, shake a wing. Jayden removes the three large rocks, throwing them as far as he can into the courtyard. Pillars of the temple, down. As soon as the bee is exposed, crouching there with its cartoon proportions and delirious antennas, Matt slams his foot down. Not satisfied with the first blow, the boys jostle to stamp the creature to death.

COUNSELLOR THOMSON was 38 and breath-taking. Fresh-faced and lean with boundless cascading chestnut hair and calm eyes like a Norwegian Fjord and effortlessly crisp white shirts and the fitted blue jeans of a professional jet-setter, or reluctant aristocrat. Her particular clean dazzle beauty emphasised the especially horrid surroundings and enervating company. Inmate William drank black coffee, the image of the sewer black liquid coursing through his mouth into his body flooded the Counsellor's mind. She found the image apt but did not smile. Breathtakingly unattractive, the swarthy gleam of the Inmate's sallow skin might have been re-cast as a Mediterranean glow were it not for two coal nuggets for eyes and thin lips which were stuck on his face like poorly crafted stop-motion animation, or old rolled leather. The sallow man drank his coffee in a bitter protest, a capsule of synthetic creamer left untouched, but not forgotten, beside him.

The meeting had drawn to a close. The Counsellor's oceanic eyes intensely focused despite the relaxed aura of her posture. "Do you have anything further you want to express?"

William the Inmate: Using up every last second of this exchange with an adult not clad in prison fatigues, and using it up with sarcasm. "Yeah, I'm an Aquarius."

Nonplussed, she of the chestnut mane savoured a long beat reviewing a collection of handwritten and printed notes. William the Inmate's irritation grew in concert with her absorption.

"If it's the about the marmite thing in the mess-" gasped the Inmate. The Counsellor's negated, her languid speech belying a sharpness in her face. "There is something we've never discussed before and I'd like to address it now."

"What?"
She leant back serenely. "From the court transcripts."

Inmate William never could suppress an urge to roll his eyes in bloody boredom, when the meagre intellects of any who sought his company had used up the last remnants of his precious patience.

"Let's sum up: not to rub salt, but just to stay present in the truth of what you did, and true to the present of what you've acknowledged. "

The same yogic nonsense. Truths and nows and space and namastes. New age rehabilitation. He wondered not for the first or twentieth time whether it was conceived to bring about a mass demand for the return of electro-shock therapy.

"Sure."

"Why are you here?"

The tired repetition of wrongs was surely in and of itself wrong.

"Because I got caught breaking The Law."

Counsellor Thomson didn't engage or recriminate. She had moved to statements, voice a practiced calm.

"I think you know that's not helpful William." She paused for effect, marking a change in tone which she had never deployed with him before. The mollifying nuances, the soft sparks of encouragement, gone.

"You're here. In prison, Sitting in that plastic seat and enduring one way conversations every week. This is what your life has become. Because you participated in the live-stream rape of a six year old child. We've had so many discussions, and you've never taken responsibility for actively participating." She scanned his eyes, not for effect, but out of curiosity. "Mindfulness. I acknowledge my own truth. A truth that I failed in bringing you into a safe space where you could own your responsibility. I forgive myself for this failure."

"Congratulations."
The Counsellor received the sarcasm with a smile.

"It's one thing to watch, but you went further than that. You intervened. You asked for the boy to smile and wave to the camera, while he was being assaulted."

William in a dead stare, the cogs failing to latch.

"I'm curious about this because there's a psychological torture aspect that the judge overlooked."

William the Uneasy shuffled in his seat. "I'm done talking."
Snapping like a carnivorous flower, the Counsellor fired off a proposition:

a) Gang rape
b) Rape by one perpetrator while being watched by a masturbating crowd c) Swift execution

"I'm not playing this."

In the millionth example of William the Off not getting the gist or reading the room right or being able to make a genuine connection, he failed to understand that the Counsellor's game was never a game and if it had been, it was surely at an end. The yogic nonsense truth and owning and responsibility and listening with soft smiles and a passive face to avert judgement was a country road that stretched for miles and miles with no one in sight except a roadhouse with a big neon welcome sign with his name on it so that when he got back to his car having expelled his junk diet into the amenities and filled up on heart-warming apple pie he could get back in the car and find the middle road to humility and respect and empathy and maybe, just maybe, love... And not run anyone down who happened to be waiting by the side of the road, minding their own business.

"You have a right to decline, and a right to choose. But the thing is, your free will always hurt others. And that is where a rule of protection must come into play." The Counsellor's eyes are searching, entrancing. As the seconds settled after these words of deliberation, her bearing changed. Something robotically factual, straight edged takes form.

"There are several lifers in here who would love to meet a paedophile. They keep a tidy collection of barbed wire. You understand. A, B or C? Would you like me to repeat?"

William the Inmate cackles through a red face. "Yeah, alright. B! How you going to arrange that then? You got a webcam up your arse?" Maniacal laughter ballooned out in front of him.

A slender foot in a polished elf-toe court shoe, soft Italian leather, kicked a bag toward him with her feet. Inside, several glowing phones. "Ready to stream, love."

The hitherto efficient normalcy of the proceedings slid sideways to surreal threat. Oh the words, glorious words which have been tipped on the tongue for months, as patient professionalism held savage contempt behind civil sighs and obtuse platitudes which she knew were utterly wasted.

"I'm your counsellor but I won't counsel you. Just as you chose to make your own laws outside I'm offering you to determine your own future in here. A, B or C."

"It's not like the kid died!"
"I think you know that I would argue that that statement is very, very subjective."

The Counsellor paused, a glint in her eyes. "Are you saying that execution is not a fitting response? Is this "no" on option c?"

The Inmate stared blankly, a mirror to his soul, finding nothing in his sluggish cogs to navigate a smug way out of this bizarre prodding. The Counsellor correctly deciphered his sparkless cognition, a benign and beatific smile spread across her exquisite face.

A timed glance to the unused creamer. "Can I get you a coffee, with real milk?"

"Sure." William the Victor. The Chestnut surely transcribed his speechlessness as strength... that sullen defence mechanism which masked mental stagnation, had come into its own. The Sallow man was suddenly smug, sebanaceous glands oozing, suddenly back in the game. The Chestnut Mare surrendered the game to a bribe. What a fall, what cheaply wrangled defeat!

Security Camera 3: 11.09am/West Quarter Female defendant walks to back of public viewing room. Unidentified female warden attending coffee urns turns at approach. Unclear of warden's actions [verification needed]. Female defendant walks back to the table to sit opposite Inmate William.

The witch's spell is broken. The supreme stoicism of the untainted ego and the supremely strong has defeated the silly and strange manipulation. William's voice drips.

"A, B or C. An eye for an eye makes the whole world blind. See, I'm learning."

William slurped the dregs. Triumph.

The Counsellor's eyes flickered to a large white clock in the meeting hall.

"You won. The real you won. The real you really won. You were never happy to go along with anyone's game. You always did exactly as pleased you."

The red face faded, the sallow reappeared, beady eyes self-satisfied and yet spiteful in victory.

"One last thing William. I want you to think of little Daniel Oxford. Not now, if you don't want. Just over the next few days. I'm going to give you some reading material."

"We've got a million bibles."

"Oh, this isn't a story." Elegant hands hand a neat collection of notes and photos. "These are fragments of Daniel's life. The hospital where he was born, a diary his mother Nadia kept when he was a baby. His favourite toys, the moment he first

learned to laugh. The nights he held onto a sweaty old jumper left by his father after he died."

Slug fingered hands raised in mockery. "You want empathy. So I off myself with remorse and 'boo boo oh dear how could I'?!"
"That's really not a requirement."

"Oh, really, it's not a **requirement**?" William mumbled, everything so tedious when the last sip has been drunk.

The Counsellor's clear and direct voice. No reason for mellifluous tones, patronising tones, the dispensation of maxims and ladling of encouragement. "An eye for an eye making the whole world blind... you know, I agree in principle. In my heart of hearts, I really do. I am a pacifist. But the world's overpopulated."

Written in a notebook: "Inmate delegated Option C, 11.11am."

William glanced up at the clock, a hair shirt on a summer morning. "Alright love, haven't got all day."

"Oh, I know." She looked at him directly. " You are not willing to experience an approximation of the crimes you committed on a vulnerable child, observed or unobserved. You will be executed. But to satisfy my own sense of justice - purely subjective here, and I own that- it won't be swift."

Oh to be rid of all this sound and fury, thinking of things good and bad and cycles of retribution and loss.

"Well I hope it's swift because I've got legal studies in 15 minutes. I'm getting a degree."

Words that a court-approved lip-syncer deduced with ease. Oh beautiful mime. The unexpectedly erotic enunciation of words in slow motion.

You are going to die very, very slowly Over the next nine days.

A collection of notes and photos pushed in front of him like a death warrant. "I could have made it faster. But I've spent a lot of time reading these."

Sceptical silence. Contemplation of a left-field psychological assessment, did he fail? Will there be ramifications? God no, not the TV. Must have the TV.

"Alright then. Thanks for the coffee."

The swish of chestnut hair over a crisp white shirt, the easy swing of a soft leather bag.

"It was honestly my pleasure."

What passed for disconcertion on the Inmate's face would appear as self-satisfaction to a common observer. When it doubt, turn on the smarm. The old smothering contrived intimacy that endeared all the mothers at park playgrounds, engendered their trust. The old clothes are shapeless now. Prison has frittered the seams, and he bristled at the pointless game, for not knowing what the point was.

"Thanks, love. Hope you had fun and got all your little boxes ticked."

The Counsellor's benevolent smile, radiant against the grey, disinfectant splashed concrete.

"You'll develop a slight fever and then lesions. When the grey spots on your wrists turn to black lines, you've got about 12 hours left. Happy reading."

Low, sharp heels clicked on the cold floor.

A ZED talk in full swing, a space blackened by darkness save for a spotlight on Dr Jan Dulac. The crowd is full, expectant. A lower third on an otherwise empty screen reads: X-CELLE BIOTECH INNOVATIONS - SAVING THE WORLD WITH SCIENCE.

Dr Dulac is neither Scandinavian nor French, but has the learned face of a polyglot and the bearing of a scientist who has a sideline in motivational speaking, which in a way, she does. Although her sideline is a one off, a one hit wonder, a crash and a bang and a clarion call and death knell. It is a hydrogen bomb of centuries of pent-up words which dared never be uttered, with revelations that burst through clouds like a millennial, neo-diluvian storm. Her words ring out like a gunshot in Sarajevo on June 28th 1914, the thud of boots marching into Poland on a bright September morning... but they carry the promise of something else too... discovery of Penicillin, a tin can called Apollo 11 floating through time and space...it is the rainbow burst of potential, the unimaginable cacophony of shrieks and exhalations from the animal kingdom as the bulldozers retreat, the collective sigh of a billion happier endings.

At the end of the ZED talk, Dr Jan Dulac sits alone on stage, waiting for the penny to drop, the escorts to come, violence to erupt. As she sits in this ecstasy of apprehension, her role fulfilled, the next steps so clear in her mind it cuts other memories like glass, she pulls out a revolver, points it to her temple, and pulls.

Her words did the trick. The fuse was lit.

Speech of Dr Jan Dulac, November 5th 2019, ZED.

Since the dawn of humanity, mankind has forced his will upon his surroundings, starting with little more than a desire to reach beyond his grasp. From living in caves to exploring space the human animal has achieved extraordinary feats, made manifest by creativity, passion, force and imagination. These accomplishments should stand as sublime monuments to an enlightened, benevolent organism, yet they are tarnished, marred by base, un-evolved instincts and instead have come to fruition not because of - but in-spite of - mankind's fundamentally violent nature. From the absolute beginning to this very moment, certain things have never changed. Rape, murder, torture, war, hate, fear, religion, ignorance, stupidity, selfishness, destruction... this unenviable list goes on and on and repeats over and over. Man has wantonly destroyed everything in his path. Even his own creations, even himself, even this fragile lifeboat which floats in the maw of an incomprehensible void. What astonishing stupidity, what flagrant hubris! The pendulum has swung so far beyond it's parabulia that mankind is faced with it's own undoing. It's tragic beyond words. But let's forget the bad for a moment. Can you imagine where the human race might be if all the death and destruction did not exist? If there was a way to end it overnight? Is it possible? How can you have the good without the bad? The Yin without Yang? Dark without light? It's impossible right? It's just human nature. Well, that is half true. If there was a way to move ahead with grace and benevolence - could we do it? Would we do it? Of course we would! Of course, we are noble and magnanimous. We strive to be our greatest selves! Of course we desire peace over war, to proceed without destruction and cruelty, ignorance and fear! Okay, how? How do we do this? How do we excise this demon? The only way to do such a thing is to first know the cause. Ah the cause, the one elegant truth which unlocks our exquisite future. What is the one common denominator that will make clear the solution? What is the cause? What is it that so disrupts our potential for empathy, love and peace? One that we can know categorically to be the cancer eroding our better selves? (pause) The answer is so painfully obvious that it's truly astonishing no one has ever realized it before. No one has realized it because of a fundamental assumption about the necessity of the whole, that the whole can only exist as such. That it cannot be without it's component parts. And this component seemed so innate and fundamental as to be a law of the universe. You see the cause is so ubiquitous and so seemingly inexorable from human nature that no one has ever questioned it's necessity. And in this grand assumption that all things are necessary, we still put a value on the component parts. We diminish the value of traits like empathy and compassion and kindness and make them synonymous with "weakness." Silly flimsy things which innately belong to the subordinate sex, we teach that those characteristics are not born of strength, but made for ridicule. In their place, we worship ego, and brute strength. Ego, and domination. These simple, two dimensional things. Things that are black, and white. Me against You. Us, and Them. And we're back to the cause again. How could we be so obtuse as to miss it? Once I've said it, you won't believe that you ever missed it, how we all could have missed it. But before I get to the cause, I'm going to show you a revolutionary creation. It's the single most important creation in human history and it's... a virus.

In video footage of the speech, it was at this point that behind JAN a large image of an inky black microscopic virus was seen to wriggle and mutate.

Today I'm going to talk to you about an organism, a tiny organism that is extremely successful. The reason why will become clear soon enough, but for now meet Heilothanpri

Chromostophene. HC is a virus, but don't worry, HC is a good virus, we like this virus, it will protect the human race from self-destruction. This virus began in a lab in 1946, and has taken seven decades of finessing by the most pioneering scientists of the last century. It is the most successful, virulent virus ever to be created in a lab. What makes a virus successful? Well a few things, adaptability, communicability, resilience and the amount of time it takes for the host to show symptoms. You can be the most virulent virus in the universe but if your host dies before they can transmit you around you might become extinct before you get a chance to keep going. So if you are 100 percent successful and you have a nice long gestation period so your host can spread you around, six months in the case of our little friend HC here, then you will be a happy little virus. Well our little friend here has a 100% mortality rate among it's hosts, 100%! It will gestate for anywhere between 12-18 months, while being infectious. Great news for HC, bad news for the host. If no symptoms present, no antibodies can be manufactured either in a lab or in nature to combat the virus, then when it does present, the host dies within four weeks. Now, you may be wondering how an unstoppable virus is good for humanity, or the host, except in this case the host is in fact the underlying cause for much human suffering. And here we are back to that question. What is the cause? That elusive cause... The flaw?

The screen behind her went black. A single light shone on JAN.

The fundamental flaw with mankind is right there in front of us... The fundamental flaw with Man... is Men.

A huge, packed and sweaty warehouse. Music pounds the walls as multi-coloured lights refract through a haze of smoke and sweat. Hundreds of bodies writhe together in a mass orgy of frenzied, deranged passion. Amongst the intertwined bodies, young men and women dance feverishly, amid foam, drugs and booze. Huge banners, glimpsed peripherally read "We Go Down Together," "Apocalypse Now." In low-lit corners of the warehouse, 'Chill Out' zones host serious faces conducting candle-lit ceremonies. Many of the people in the chambers appear to not be moving.

Nimh walks quickly. Earphones in, music obliterating all else, she wears a hoodie, cutting an androgynous figure amongst the largely empty streets. Something grovels in the street ahead, the stick insect outline of an emaciated heroin addict, arms outstretched. The forearms are black, and appear as burnt twigs. Nimh crosses to the other side of the suburban street. It isn't time for horror just yet, the song hasn't

finished and she is carried away by the emotion of the song, smudged kohl eyeliner and specks of glitter graze her face.

Spying from the top storey of a 1930s terraced house, Rohan carefully surveys the landscape. At the sight of Nimh breezing down the street his lips purse.

It is an overcast day in Sussex as Nimh closes the door behind her; flicking not one but three locks. She is folding her earphones into her pocket when Rohan appears at the top of the stairs.

"Don't bother hiding them. I saw you from the window." His voice is soft but righteous.

"Were you spying on me?"

"Why would you break a promise? I didn't raise you to lie. Do you want to be attacked?"

Nimh is suddenly exhausted. "Dad, I have eyes."

"You need all your bloody senses! You don't know who could be around the-" before he can finish, Rohan coughs violently, the air expelled out of his chest like a storm. Nimh dashes forward but Rohan manages to shake her off."I'm fine, I'm fine."

As he straightens up, very faint grey spots are visible on his forearms. Nimh notices and pales before correcting herself.

"I'm sorry. I just put them in when the house was in sight. Promise." "How was X-Celle?"

"Fine. C'mon, I'll make some tea." As Nimh walks through to the kitchen, she hears the droll intoning of a newsreader on the television:

Since the first outbreak in March at Rorehilde Prison at which convicted pedophile William Brockhurst was identified as the UK's Patient Zero, so called vigilante rape and death squads targeting women and girls as young as-

Nimh turns to her father. "This is what you're worried about?" She switches off the television angrily. "Me?"

"There have been three squad attacks in Brighton in the past two days." Rohan senses Nimh's dismissiveness. "Nimh! A twelve year girl was hacked to death by a squad in Somers Street Park. That's 3 miles from here!"

Nimh slams the kettle down. "Dad, I get it! They can't get anywhere near X-Celle, we've got a fucking paramilitary unit."

Rohan looks like he is going to break. His daughter doesn't notice, back to the task of making tea.

Nimh is in her room, changing from plain black clothes into ripped jeans and a rainbow coloured jumper. She flicks on music and turns on her computer. Emails from 'X-Celle' flash up, coding homework. A score reveals 70.3 'under review.' Nimh grimaces at it, moving the mouse to read the whole email. Her face scrunched up in irritation, she clicks off the screen; a sound scuffling outside captures her attention.

Moving to the window but staying safely behind the curtain, she sees movement at the house opposite. The house has about five cars jammed in the driveway and on the pavement, a re-purposed ambulance flashes in the street as a body is removed from the house.

A young woman in an oversized woollen jumper is on her knees in the front garden, sobbing. It is a disturbing sight, and Nimh is not immune to it.

As the doors of the re-purposed van close, the woman gets up, shakily locking the front door before shoving a suitcase into a car at the front of the driveway. She gives a long lingering look at the house, gets in the car, and drives away without a backwards glance.

Nimh is lost in the sudden conclusion of the desolate scene, and is jolted by a knock at the door as ROHAN enters.

"Darling, can we have a quick chat?" Nimh nods, gesturing for him to come in.

She indicates toward the door, "they just cleared out Number 11. The girlfriend left. "

Rohan's eyes are heavy as he acknowledges the news silently.

"Maybe we should take one of the cars." Rohan gives a look of distaste. "Dad, they're just going to sit there. "

"Let's leave it a few days. There may be relatives."

They sit on her bed. Nimh's room is a curious mix of high-end technology, fluffy unicorns and grunge band posters; a relic of a happier time, and hopelessly anachronistic now.

Rohan takes a breath. "I thought it might be a nice idea to have Gran and Julia over for supper tomorrow night." Sensing what's coming next, Nimh springs up agitated.

"Dad, I can't. I've got too much work to do. I'm slipping behind as it is."

"What do you mean you're slipping behind?"
Nimh looks sheepish but is quick enough to deflect it. "My average sank. It's fine, I can get it back up."

Rohan is genuinely crestfallen. "You love the program Nimh."
"Yeah well it's a bit of a challenge feeling inspired at the moment." "Why?"

"Why do you think?"

Rohan thinks for a long beat. "Don't blame the program darling. They're trying to prepare you as best as possible. They will be your future." Her father's calm consideration is not what Nimh needed, and as usual, she uses his placidity as a springboard for adolescent rage.

"Dad! Jesus. Seriously? Where is your anger? I didn't sign up for this! NO ONE DID!"

"I know darling. But something had to change."
"Not like this!"
"We were staring down the barrel of atomic annihilation, I would gladly sacri-"

"Okay okay. I can't argue about it again. I'm just not going to give my all to an organisation that has lied to me since I was 12. Don't worry, I won't flunk out, but don't expect me to be a smiling assassin robotically building their femtopia."

"Don't think of it as a, utopia, Nimh. It's just a chance. It's a chance for the planet to survive. For peace to survive. For you to-"

"I know, I know Dad - fine. I can't - you want to have this Supper, go for it. But I can't sit through it."

"Let's not fight. Please."

The silence in the room is oppressive; words teeming to be said aloud. Both sit there stiffly.

"I want you to know that I have no regret. No anger. My only priority is getting you safely through the next three months." Rohan's earnestness silences Nimh's pent-up indignation and terror. She looks at her father, thin shoulders gracing an upright

posture that looks like it takes energy to uphold. His quietly dignified face, creased with years of hard work and paternal responsibility. Taking this in, seeing these qualities as though meeting him for the first time, levels her, hinting at a maturity that she has been avoiding.

"They're thinking of arming a few of us, temporarily."

"With what?"
"I dunno Dad, but we're probably a bit past pepper spray."
"Would you be one of the "Few"?"
"Probably not. I might have missed the last few urban defence classes."

Rohan is dumbfounded. "What do you mean?"
Nimh opens the door and heads downstairs. Teenage righteousness returned.

"It's just overload Dad! Coding, ag, finance, defence - they want us there all fucking day and night!"

Rohan is hot on her trail, pale and shaken. His voice is strong in spite of it.
"Nimh Clara Singh! You stop and listen to me right now."Nimh turns by the banister.

"None of this is worth it if you carry on with this - unspeakable nonchalance. What could be more important then defence?"
Nimh looks sullenly at her feet.
"Answer me! Or I will schedule my appointment for tomorrow if you don't tell me!" Perspiration is breaking through the surface of Rohan's skin.

"Okay, settle down. I get it. I'll go. I'll go tomorrow."
Hoping the matter is settled, Nimh doesn't notice Rohan's subdued but pained expression. "Where were you?"
"When?"
"Last night!"
Nimh sheepishly looks down, rapidly trying to think up a plausible answer.
She reluctantly mumbles, "Nero's Hill."
"What is that?"
Nimh whips her head up and moves off, shaking her hands in irritation. "It's just a hang for all of my friends and friends I'll never know to celebrate the joy of life and togetherness before it all ends." Rohan is dumbfounded.
"You mean, you were there with boys, with men?"
"Friends Dad..."

"I..." Rohan coughs violently again, specks of blood on his shirt and hands. Nimh rushes forward. He waves her back. "No. Get away. I... How could you be so stupid? So reckless? I cannot lose my life knowing that you are recklessly endangering yours. Do not do that me! If you have any love, any respect for me you...at least try to love

yourself as I love you. What would your mother say? What would she think of me if I failed to protect-" Breathless, exhausted and sobbing, Rohan sinks down.
"Okay Dad, I'm sorry, I'm sorry. I'll go tomorrow, I will." Nimh takes Rohan's hand.

Rohan stares into the bathroom mirror, eyes bloodshot, skin pale. Outside we hear a window being smashed, a car alarm bleats loudly in response.

The mirror reflects an unadulterated view of his physical deterioration. While Nimh sleeps soundly, the house is still. Relieved from the well-worn charade of being a responsible parent in these brief, quiet moments, Rohan can see himself for the man he has become, the man who he never became and the man he was. In the silence of the cool morning, the full force of the unbearable predicament hits him.

Nimh is eating toast in the kitchen. She smiles as Rohan comes down the stairs and appears in the doorway. He is dressed as though going to work, in a well-cut suit and collared shirt. His face is serious and pale but his eyes shine brightly.

"You are the very definition of work ethic Dad." She teases him lovingly. His indefatigable integrity, his crisply cut suit. "I thought you could walk me into X- Celle. Defence starts in 30. And then maybe we could hang out, cook for Gran and everyone tonight."

Rohan hesitates slightly before answering but Nimh doesn't notice. He watches her carefully, pepping up to reply, "Okay, yes. That'd be great. I'll take you, but I'll pop into work for a few. Let them know."

Nimh raises her eyebrows, "Okay."

Rohan pours a glass of juice but barely sips it as Nimh grabs a hoodie makes her way to the door. "Call it clairvoyance, or just my singular ability to anticipate your determination to go into that boring badger set you call 'The Office', but I made you lunch to take in." She finds her keys on the window sill.

Rohan glances at a wrapped sandwich, banana and piece of flapjack on the counter, a heavy look.
Nimh is hovering by the door, double-checking her bag. "It's right there, next to the fridge!"

Rohan is prodded out of his reverie. "Thanks love- I'll try and make sure the badgers don't eat it first. "

Moving to the table, he pulls out an envelope with Nimh's name handwritten on it, and a box in a top cupboard with official documents. Title Deeds, passports.

"Dad! We've got to go."

Rohan gives a last look at the house as he moves to join her, placing a letter on the window sill. He is still catching one last sight of it as the doors close.

A surreal stillness possesses the streets as Nimh and Rohan walk. Although no more than a few months has passed since the world abruptly reckoned with its new fate, people have readily adopted a certain purposeful, head-down stride. Men and women - if visible - looks indistinguishable from one another, for women, it is a matter of survival. Few people stop to gawk or shy away from the sight of shrivelled corpses, exposed arms revealing what looks like burned skin and withered bones.

For the most part, a certain dread wariness manifests with the floating sensation of movement on the peripheries of sight: Curtains flutter in top storeys of homes as residents peep out, ground floors abandoned in favour of terrain with stronger sight- lines and defences. Homes quickly adapted to be vanguards of what little life is left. Some homes are already depleted of their male residents, and mild looting has already begun. Generally a sense of futility on the part of male looters prevents absolute chaos, and females desist for futility's sake as well - stores of available goods will be plentiful in three months' time, if they can just steer clear of the vengeful diseased.

The occasional car zooms past without stopping at corners. People cross the road at sight of others approaching, lost in the march to survival, and making the most of what is left.

Nimh and Rohan are used to walking in silence, in spite of the surreal slowness of their surroundings.

"Do you remember Southbar Lagoon?"

Nimh glances at her father. "Sort of. Where Mum used to take me?"

"Yes."

"What about it?"

"That sounds... difficult to believe."

"She used to take you down every day in the summer. You loved it, splashing and shrieking, even when it got chilly. You were delighted at the bubbles the water made."

Rohan's voice is gentle and Nimh listens carefully. The earnestness unnerves her. "How times change." Rohan is anchored to the memory.

"Bubbles... that word always makes me happy. It was one of your first words you know." He almost loses himself, the memory's warmth rising into his eyes, until another one causes them to harden. "One day an older boy ran up to you, this tiny blub of a baby, wobbling on newfound feet...and deliberately pushed you backwards. So hard. Your mother said you fell like you were free-falling off a cliff, hands and arms outstretched as your face was submerged under water. She had recurring dreams of that moment. It must have just been a second - but you were frozen in that eternity of helplessness in her dreams, forever."

Nimh listens intently.

"After that, things changed. She said you weren't like the other kids, splashing with abandon, even when you grew confident on your feet, running and jumping so early. We went down on a busy Saturday once, so I could see. Do you remember what you did? (she shakes her head) You spent almost the whole time with a watering can, methodically taking water from the centre of the pool, transporting it to a drain on the dry edges. Bit by bit, draining the depths. Such a face... pure seriousness, carefully supervising the water cascading through the iron slots, bubbling and vanishing. And then you'd return to the depths, fill up the little blue can, and start all over again. Like it was your duty."

Nimh is quietly listening. They stop at the gates of an imposing Brutalist building, an armed guard stands in the shadows of electronic gates.
"Sounds like a very futile enterprise. I was a weird kid."
Rohan pushes her hood back, face wracked with emotion, and kisses her cheek hard.

"Your mother and I have loved you with every breath in our bodies."

The short burst of an electronic bell bursts behind them. Several women walk hurriedly through the gates, all clad in neutral, dark clothing. Rohan's wide eyes soak in the sight of Nimh. Her intelligent and graceful oval face, inquisitive eyes always sparkling with a mischievous glint. He soaks up the young woman she has become, tall, strong, fearless. Barely blinking. But Nimh's attention is on the clatter of movement, the pull of the tribe.

"Off you go."

Nimh stops and steps closer to her father. "See you later. Love you Dad." She gives him a quick hug and smiles. Rohan watches as she disappears into the melee.

Nimh sits on a pew outside a hall. A long line of women wait attentively while ranks go in and out, checked off by an attendant, an athletic looking man with a tablet. The dull staccato of gunshots perforate the silence. Each of the women holds standard issue anti-noise ear protectors.

Sitting amongst the ranks of plainly clothed women, Nimh seems different. Without Rohan, a hard, steel look cloaks her eyes, the adolescent outrage replaced by a grittier cynicism.

She is deep in thought, looking down at her hands. Sarah, a young woman sitting next to her, shuffles with boredom. "If they're so worried about us, why don't they just keep us in a high security building until every last man is dead?"

When she answers, even the tone in Nimh's voice is changed. Deeper, flatter - without the sardonic, undulating melody of drama she reserves for her father.
"Because that wouldn't be practical."
"Really? What are we looking at? Another three months max? If they run out of food the para unit could go and re-stock. Better than having to sleep with a Glock under your pillow."

"They're giving us Glocks?"

Sarah is incredulous. "Didn't you come to assignment session?" Irritation and disappointment crosses Nimh's face. "They want us to sleep with one eye open Sarah. That's the point."

"I don't think the Program wants women, babies and girls to be raped and murdered by a bunch of psycho dudes who are about to die. There is no future without us. X- Celle's not trying to destroy the world Nimh, they're fucking saving it."

Nimh looks down, not sure whether she should bother to engage.

"It's not an overlooked detail, and it's not a lack of preparation. If the Program wanted to shift all of us into secure buildings until the disease works through every last man on the planet, they could. And they would have. (beat) They anticipated the reaction. They want us to remember why they're doing what they're doing. The base root of Man. Murder, Violence. We will watch - and maybe - die on the frontline so our own personal losses don't overwhelm us, overwhelm the cause. Because then we would all be fucked."

Sarah is dumbstruck.

"It's not just Men who will be sacrificed."

The two sit in heavy silence. One of the women next to Sarah is called up, placing ear protectors on as she rises. Sarah shifts in her seat. "That your Dad at the Gates?" "Yep."

"He's still working?"

"Yep."

Sarah takes this in. "Wow."

Nimh jolts in her seat, "He didn't take his lunch-" She jumps up, drops the ear protectors and sprints out.

Agile and lean, Nimh runs flat out, stopping only to look up the street both ways - figure out which direction to go. The world spins as adrenaline pounds her heart. She gambles on turning left. Home.

The house is undisturbed as NIMH bursts in. Her voice echoes the stillness. "DAD????"
Nimh frantically flips through the rooms at the front of the house. No sign of him. In the kitchen, the packed lunch sits on the table untouched.
Running upstairs to Rohan's bedroom, Nimh runs to his desk. It is tidy up and empty of everything except his diary. A letter sticks out of its edges. She pulls it out, revealing NHS letterhead. Nimh's hands shake as the words float before her eyes: "CONFIRMATION OF APPOINTMENT: DIGNATORIUM."

The creased paper reads: "You have elected to receive end of life treatment at the Sussex Dignatorium on Thursday, 9th March at 10.15am. Please call 01273-"

Nimh blanches and races downstairs. The kitchen clock reads 09.47am. In a swift, instinctive movement, Nimh pulls open a cupboard door under the stairs and grabs a hammer from a large tool bag. She slams the door behind her. In the kitchen, Rohan's lunch sits in the still kitchen, made with love, ominously untouched. As she races to leave she sees the letter on the window sill, she grabs it.

Barely looking from side to side, Nimh runs over to Number 11, the now deserted scene of last night's tearful scene. Four cars are still parked outside, the house is locked up. In a single, forceful sweep, Nimh smashes a window in. Opening the door she enters, finding a bowl of car keys in the hall. She frantically presses the buzzers until a car responds. A reciprocal beep from a blue sedan. Nimh scrambles to the driver's side and tears down the road, letter in hand. She doesn't bother stopping at the end of the road, gunning through mainly empty streets. The clock ticks 09.53am.

A beautiful Victorian house with a circular driveway, a large, improvised car-park sits in an adjacent field. A sealed off area is just visible at the back, the tops of two trucks appear to be the central activity in the area.

The Sussex Dignatorium.

A large waiting room with men of all ages sitting alone, or waiting with family. Religious representatives are sprinkled among the waiting. A Rabbi sits with a small family, sharing a tale, laughter is forced through desperate faces. Last moments of joy. A Priest solemnly holds a Bible with another man, they trace the words with their fingers quietly. Families and spouses hold hands, knuckles white. Some sob, others sit staring vacantly.

NIMH looks around. A large clock on the wall reads: 10.07am. She races to the front desk, a male receptionist looks up.

"I'm looking for Rohan Singh. Dark skin, 5'10 - he has an appointment at 10.15--- I'm his daughter."

The Receptionist scans through a list on his computer. "10.15am...Singh..."

The clock ticks. Nimh looks around desperately, two swinging doors are sealed shut. As a Nurse beeps through, Nimh makes a break for them, pushes past the startled Nurse. Ignoring the commotion she scans the corridors.

"DAD!!!"

Branching off the main corridor are well-furnished living rooms with views of the outside gardens. Nimh scans them, vision blurred by adrenaline. At the end of the

corridor, she stops at the sight of a suited figure, standing straight, silhouetted by the light outside. A humble, dignified pose. Even from the back, it is unmistakably Rohan.

"Dad!" Nimh rushes towards him. "Have they done it? What have you taken?" She sweeps toward him. "How could you go without telling me? Dad?"
Nimh is shaking.
"Darling..."

"Dad, please, please... leave with me - we have to go right now-"
An exhausted looking Nurse and Security Guard have arrived at the door. The Nurse has a patient face but feels every minute of her double shift.

"Is everything okay here?

"Yes, yes, I'm sorry. This is my daughter."

"...Okay Mr Singh.... You didn't nominate a witness so she will have to wait outside until we have her processed-"

Nimh glares at Rohan. "Please Dad, I don't care what comes next." Her tone is beseeching. "I won't fight without you."

Rohan looks at her, emotion swelling but held back.

"Okay, okay." He fights the flood of emotion and addresses the Nurse. "I'm sorry, I'm forfeiting my spot."

The Nurse looks sympathetically at the two. "Of course, you'll need to sign out and I have to advise that you may lose the opportunity to re-book." Nimh has grabbed Rohan's arm and is already frogmarching him out.

"He's not re-booking."

The living room is tidy, the soft amber glow of lamps warm. Nimh and Rohan clasp cups of tea. Uneaten biscuits sit before them. Nimh breaks the silence.

"You left me a fucking letter?"

After a life spent mitigating the abrasions of confrontation, mollifying antagonists or changing the subject, retreating into passivity, Rohan stands firm.

"I didn't want your last memory of me to an argument." He braces himself. "I'm holding you back Nimh. I anchor you to your childhood, the old world. It's time for you to join the new. I am terrified you are going to get left behind. The best thing... and the worst thing... is that you are always going to be my little girl. And I will always be your Daddy. I want to go out on my terms, not dragging you down in the horror of what will come. You need to embrace the future. Before it's too late."

Nimh sits for a long time. Taking it all in.

"I understand Dad. I do. I won't get left behind. But I'm not having you go early. I won't accept that. As long as you're alive there's a chance. I know you've given up, but I haven't. Maybe there's a cure? Maybe not everyone gets it? You're not even that sick

yet!" Rohan averts his eyes, her face questioning and the familiar tone of indignation returning to her voice. "I've got to get back to the program." She looks at him searchingly. "They already issued weapons."

Nimh fidgets in the armchair, unwilling to leave. Rohan senses her wariness.
"I don't have a second appointment. I promise." Rohan meets her eyes, smiling. "They find most patients don't need them." Nimh looks at him, unable to appreciate the joke. Eyes huge wells of pain. She rubs her face, takes a deep breath.
"Alright. I'll head out." The movement resets her, the resolve brightening her face. She goes to the uneaten lunch. Flops it down in front of him.
"At least this won't go to waste."

NIMH brushes her hair and gets a jumper, readying herself to go out. On her desk, her phone and email flash with a red alert "GANGS, call 333". Underneath the alert is a map with a red dot radiating in bursts. Nimh doesn't notice, grabbing a scarf. Her eyes catch a photo on her desk, her parents with a baby, big brown eyes beaming. The sight of it knocks the wind out of her chest. She sinks down beside her bed, scrunching her body up tight, losing herself in the abyss.

A huge crash rocks the street outside. Snapping her head up, Nimh springs up and turns off the lamp. Moving to the window she carefully spies through a gap in the curtains: a group of men surround a house. They have smashed a car into the front door and windows of a house up the road; splintering it's heavily fortressed door. Within minutes a woman has been dragged out, screaming for her life. She is utterly defenceless as she is stabbed to death by a gang of frenzied attackers. As her limbs cease to flail her body is dropped carelessly onto the ground. Most of the men enter the house but one hangs back, circling the woman's body. With barely a glance over his shoulder, he pulls her toward him and starts to rape her.

Nimh watches, frozen.
"Nimh. Get away from the window."
Rohan slowly approaches, Nimh doesn't move.
The woman is lying motionless in the garden. As the rest of the gang move on to the next door, one of the men comes out of the house, carrying a female child. Indistinct yells from the group sound as Nimh averts her eyes, moving toward her

Dad.

"I've got to call the Unit. I can't take them on alone. They're ramming. I think we should go."

"We can't. There could be gangs everywhere!"

"They're isolated groups Dad, but they're going door to door, they'll be sweeping streets - I counted 7, 7 or 8. We have to just go, out the back."

Nimh grabs her phone to call for help, sees the red dot flash slowly. As she holds it in her hand other dots appear. All in close proximity. A banner starts to scroll "Coordinated group attacks. Run, hide, attack. REPORT IN 333 keep location pin ON."

Rohan sees the message. "Pack a bag. Now. We're going to Ruthglen."

"What about the girl?" Nimh moves toward the curtain in an agony of dread. "Stop Nimh. It is too late! Did they arm you?" Nimh looks sick with guilt. He is right. She starts frantically packing a big backpack.

"Get the kitchen knives. I'll take the cricket bat."

Rohan springs to action. "Good god!"

The sound of the raiding gang intensifies, Rohan periodically checks the front windows - there are more men now, as though a new group has merged. They are less than three houses away.

Grabbing what food he can, the vital documents from the kitchen, a photo and a large bottle of water, he stashes a few last things and slips out the back door. Nimhis waiting, looking up at her childhood home one last time. They lock the door and climb the fence in the back garden, cutting through the neighbour's back yard to the next street.

Nimh and Rohan pace through the suburban streets, pulling over in the shadows along a wooden fence hung with ivy. The sound of alarms ring out as POLICE and an X- CELLE RESPONSE UNIT zoom past. The sounds of anarchic yelling, bloodlust and cars ramming intensify. Not moving an inch, Rohan and Nimh wait and listen.

Rohan whispers urgently, "Maybe we should wait for the unit to clear them... and go back, get a plan together for the morning."
"We should just get out of here. We've got a plan. North."
"Maybe you could go in tomorrow, get issued a weapon- you're going to get in trouble if you don't report in-"

"That attack was coordinated. It's more important that we stay together. Let's just go to the cabin. We need to get you somewhere... We need a car. A good one."
Rohan takes the lead. "Follow me. Stay close."

Nimh switches her phone off. The two walk furtively underneath a train station. The tunnel is of post-WW2 construction, weathered brown bricks and simple, sturdy curves. Scrawls of neon graffiti scar its surface. A long fluorescent light flickers as they pass through to the other side. Once the bottle neck is safely behind them, Nimh keeps look-out for a suitable car. The street is deathly quiet, curtains tightly drawn, cars parked erratically on the street. Many have smashed windows.

As they approach a residential intersection, a gang of tall men appears out of nowhere. Knives and jerry rigged weapons in hand, faces obscured by balaclavas. Oddly, some of the figures wear Islamic veils, the figures they hide underneath distinctly male. Nimh and Rohan freeze in a moment that seems to last an eternity. A huge man in his forties is at the head of the gang, a blue balaclava covers his face. He carries a steel bat, though hardly looks like he would need it.

When he speaks, his voice is commanding and urgent. "D'you come from the Shoreham Rd?" Nimh and Rohan have time to take stock; the Gang has a few women in it. Nimh is stunned.
Rohan responds, "Yes, yes we did, just now."
"How many of the cunts were there?"
Nimh steps forward, "About 8 - they're fast, they've got knives. A woman was dragged out, they killed her...then they took a girl-"
A masculine voice inside exclaims, "Fuck that!" In total synchronicity the Gang plunge forward, running in the direction of Nimh's home. The burly leader looks over his shoulder at the slight figures of Nimh and Rohan and yells. "Find a garden shed and hide!"

Nimh and Rohan are shaky with relief and keep moving, fast. Nimh sees a car with a window down but not smashed in; a mid-2000s Audi. She nudges Rohan to look at it, veering towards the road. He tugs her back and points forward. Trusting his lead, they continue. At the end of the road they approach a private cul-de-sac. On the left is an elegant driveway, a newish Land Rover Discovery is parked there, untouched.

As Rohan walks around the back of the car to the side of the house, Nimh pulls on his sleeve, whispering urgently, "Dad, stop - the alarms on these things."
"It's Alan's car."
"Alan! He's not going to let you take it!" Rohan doesn't respond, just keeps walking purposefully until he at the side of a large Georgian terrace. He flattens his hands on the window to see if it's open. It's stuck in its wooden frame, old paint and twisted vines tangling it shut. Summoning a strength that will take a toll on him later, Rohan manages to get a grip, prying it up.

"Dad, we can't steal his car. Jesus."
"Quiet!" With some difficulty, Rohan has pried open the casing of the window, wedging it open. He motions for Nimh to come over and gives her a leg up. Once inside she looks around to see if anyone is there before in turn pulling him in. Rohan scrabbles to get over the ledge, as Nimh whispers to him. "What now?"
High ceilings and navy blue Farrow and Ball paint frame the interior, a classical scene interrupted by bold contemporary art and black and white photographs, masculine erotica. Rohan walks around the house quietly, but with confidence. He looks for car keys at the front entrance. There's nothing but a wallet. He takes out the credit card and cash. Nimh sees, stunned by this uncharacteristic move, "Dad!"
Rohan goes to the kitchen, a ceiling to floor wine rack of rare

and valuable reds and white in one corner, the brushed steel bench top spotless, save a solitary glass of half- drunk red wine. Rohan walks through to the conservatory, rich with terrariums, ferns and the deliberate chaos of an authentic Victorian conservatory. The space is bathed in moonlight, casting a silvery glow on potted plants, a dusty rose, velvet-cloaked chaise-longue and a telescope.

As Nimh reaches the doorway, she sees Rohan kneeling by the recliner. Silver light glows off the death mask of a man, skin porcelain, eyeballs glistening toward the moon. Alan's arms are covered in fine pink cashmere, but his fingers have turned

black. Rohan leans over his friend and whispers into his ear quietly, before gently shutting his glassy eyes.

Nimh stares.
Rohan gets up and moves to the kitchen, opens a drawer near the fridge. The car keys.

He turns to Nimh. "Find blankets, water, food..." Nimh nods assent.
"Bring it to the front but don't open the door. Hurry."
Nimh looks up at her father curiously as he moves out of the kitchen, "What are you getting?"
Rohan looks back over his shoulder. "Books, cashmere and red wine."
"Dad! Towels, deodorant and toothpaste. Trust me."

Outside, Rohan and Nimh stealthily pack the car. When they are finished, Rohan shuts the front door and goes to the driver's seat.

"Dad, I should drive."

Rohan sets his jaw in determination. "No one cares about a dead man." Nimh reels. "Don't say that. If the roads are bad I should be behind the wheel. Dad. C'mon, I'll wear my hoodie."

Rohan exhales and looks doubtful. "Okay, but I'll get us out of town. You can take over when we reach the A27."

Nimh reluctantly gets in the passenger seat as Rohan starts the car. She folds a huge woollen blanket over her shoulders and hunkers down. She can just about see Rohan's hands gripping the wheel but not much else. "How much petrol have we got?"

Rohan edges through the suburban streets, driving at a cautious pace. "It's full." Nimh raises her head, getting one last glimpse of the Georgian terrace as it's ghostly elegance retreats into the distance.

Under her breath, whisper. "Thank you Alan."

The car makes its way through the coastal streets, headlights off. As they peel out onto a dual carriageway a police car flashes by, followed by an unmarked van - an X- Celle paramilitary vehicle.

Rohan slows to a respectful distance. "I hope we're doing the right thing."

Nimh is sitting up in the back, anxious to lead the journey. "We are."

They are leaving the suburban roads behind them as they twist up a side road to the highway.

"I don't think the gangs were supposed to be this bad." Nimh searches the darkness outside. "They weren't just arming a few of us today. I think they were arming everyone."

Rohan shoots her a sharp glance. "Did you manage to..."

Nimh looks at her Dad admonishingly. "I was too busy hijacking a car and rescuing you from the goddamned pound."

They approach a roundabout fringed by semi-rural land. There are no cars, the night is still until out of the darkness an emaciated man staggers in front of the car. His arms are black and his face a grotesquely cavernous assembly of sinew and bone. Rohan swerves the car.

"Dad, GO!"

Rohan corrects, bumping over a curb and back onto the road. The Man lies on the asphalt behind them, twisted and inert under the moonlight. Rohan anxiously looks back.

Nimh sees his distress. "Okay, pull over."

Rohan stops the car, heart racing, as Nimh climbs over and they switch seats. Nimh adjusts the seat and they continue in silence, taking the freeway.

Rohan's voice is shaky. "Nimh, please. Put your hoodie up."

They drive in silence as the fields grow longer, leaving the South-East behind.

Divide and conquer. Fences, gates, power lines and driveways, splitting and splintering the land's seamless tapestry. Lampposts loom over the long road, showering an artificial glare of insect-strewn light on the motorway.

Adrenaline, exhaustion. A lone car on a long road nearing London. "We should switch on the radio. See if there are any reports."
The flicker of static.
"Not too loud. I need to keep my senses."

Sporadic voices, swells of music; the deranged repetition of over-produced boy. Others frequencies are just static, until the crisp confident voice of a young man rings through the car.

"- down a notch and take the broader view. Zoom out the lens of history and you'll realise this is just a correction. Every generation in history has served up it's young men to be sacrificed in battle. It's a population cull that Men have enabled and participated in since the dawn of time. The last global culls - and we're talking WW1 and WW2 here, shed about 20 million and then 50-80 million lives. Both conflicts were separated by a miniscule 20 years! We have not had global conflict of that scale in nearly a century, and with advances in medical technology and science we are in unchartered waters population wise."

"Dad, can you pass the water?" Thin hand reaching, a hoodie slips.

"-What we do know, is that when you force people to live in "stress" conditions, i.e, Without adequate space and resources, violent criminal behaviour soars. But that's getting away from the War story onto the Environmental story. And it's the War story that is more critical right now; our viewpoint is that a natural "War Cull" is inevitable, and I think recent provocations by nuclear states makes that obvious. As another War Cull appears unstoppable - a cull which would drag in innocent civilians and the environment with unparalleled devastation, the Chemical Cull - our Program - was initiated in defence of, quite literally, the planet."

The black, open road.

Another voice, strident.
"It's a radically demagogic plan. You're playing God, aren't you?"

"Men have been playing God in every decision to invade, conquer and legislate other people's freedoms since the dawn of time. It is not a question of destruction - that is an omnipresent reality of life. This is about creating the only viable chance for humanity - and yes that includes men - to survive."

A car zooming up the outside lane. Wind blown thinning hair, flat against a scalp, mouth arced like a gulping fish, bellowing into the night. A maniacal sketch of pain and exhilaration. A hoodless face exposed. Long dark strands of hair framing an elfin face. A ram, a swerve and Nimh dodges the hit, braking hard. He overcorrects, swings across lanes like a wayward Tonya Harding. Red brake lights glows.

"...these are huge, some would say abstract notions, what if there's no nuclear war? There is compelling evidence that the environment is on a slow track to - if not recovery, then stabilisation."

A burst of laughter. "Sorry, there is no evidence that retaining the environmental status quo - which in refuse alone means over 8 million tonnes of plastic enters the water each year- means stablisation."

Thin-hair starts to reverse.

"Nimh..."
"Dad... His car's a bucket of shit compared to this."

"...animal extinction, climate events... The environmental question is one of greedy self-interest groups bringing about a slow-burn extinction event for human beings - and every form of life on this planet. In our view, this leads to only one avenue of correction."

Burns off and burn out, the smell of rubber in the air, as heavy as relief is light. "You didn't have your hood up."

Two cars on the road, a discreet hunt.
"Better to have his taillights in sight. If they disappear, keep an eye on the hidden shoulder."

The radio presenter's voice fills the silence. "Surely there is more than one avenue of correction, as you said, huge leaps in science"

"-Are completely meaningless with the clear and present danger of a nuclear war. Invoking history seems to offend you but I'm going to bring it into context again, there are a couple of vital factors here. When we're looking at WW1, the ratio of deaths was only 10% civilian; by WW2 that had jumped to 50/50. In recent conflicts, the ratio is directly inverted: 90% of deaths are now civilian. We have changed how we do War. And now with the question of nuclear annihilation, this statistic is going to shift again. The guys pressing the Red Button are safe in their towers. Let's be real about what this means."

"But that's still conjecture - no one knows where a nuclear strike would hit, even the guys pushing the red button-"

"And they're always "Guys", aren't they? Listen, we're talking about a corrective measure that will last for two generations, replicating the generational effect of the last two global wars. This will almost completely even out over time, giving the planet a chance to recover and for humanity to decide how to proceed with the responsible management of our environment and our use of weapons against each other."

"For women to decide you mean. As a man, you seem to have no love lost for mankind."

The respondent laughs. "Yeah, we get that a lot. The thing is...to appropriate Shakespeare here... It's not that I loved mankind less, it's just that I loved humanity, more."

The car trails the distant red lights, in silence.

Rohan closes the fuel cap and makes his way to the petrol station to pay. Nimh is sitting in the driver's seat, face down and hoodie up.
The petrol station sits like a beacon in the pouring rain. Rohan hurries under the broad parapet to reach the shop, pushing the door open softly. A lone man sits at the counter. He is elderly, with an ashed-out cigarette in his mouth. He jerks his head up as Rohan approaches as though reluctantly leaving a dream. The shop is threadbare, every row of empty shelves a stark symbol. Sporadically left on a few shelves are gallons of engine oil, some confectionary, bags of crisps and car air fresheners.

Rohan grabs a couple of remaining chocolate bars and approaches the counter. "Morning."
In a thick Northern accent, the attendant barks out a price, barely looking up. "£70.12."

Rohan is flustered, "The meter said £50-"
"£70.12."
Rohan takes in the old man's hard bitten face, lined with deep crevices.
"No problem." Rohan passes the cash, catching a glimpse of the man's arms. "No marks?"
For the first time the man looks up at Rohan. His blue eyes

bloodshot but sharply focused. "Oh, I'll get 'em soon enough. But I've already got emphysemia, so..." The Man shrugs.

"Well, sir, I admire your work ethic. You have helped us - me, on my journey. Which will probably be my last."

The man looks at him steadily, his face slightly softened. "You got daughters?" Rohan hesitates.

"Yeah, you do. I've got three. Can't let 'em starve. And can't have them in here. They'll be working enough when it's all over for us."

There is a sense of camaraderie between them, and Rohan leans forward, his face earnest. "Are you getting vigilante gangs up here?"

The man stiffens. "Aye."

Anxiety tightens Rohan's face.

The Man notices. "Steer clear of... well...I'd go to the Highlands myself. But with four of us. Nowhere to go."

The men share a moment, there is nothing to say. Rohan places another £100 on the counter.

"Good luck to you and your daughters sir."

The man takes the cash, glances over at the Land Rover where Nimh is hiding out of sight.

"And to you and yours."

Dawn promises to break to full light as the soft landscapes of Northern England become stark, jagged. The greens and browns of the moors have de-saturated to purples and greys... the skies grey and thunderous. Nimh and Rohan are hurtling through the Scottish borders.

Rohan looks out at the low stone walls and boundless florets of heather sweeping the landscape. "Your mum and I would always play a game, to see who could guess most accurately the moment we'd pass onto Scottish land."
"How could you know without GPS?"

"We'd count the miles on the odometer and match them with the nearest sign, and then reference the car map."
"Wow. Olden days.

"It was part of the fun. We'd never agree of course. So we'd usually spend our first night in the cabin arguing about it and rehashing it with the map."

Nimh chuckles, "Sounds terrible Dad."
"Nah. It was lovely. "
Nimh looks in the rear-view mirror, no cars in sight, just endless land.
"Did you guess just now? "
"Unfortunately, I have the new map." Rohan holds his smart phone aloft, showing the direction of travel in a blue line.
"Jesus, turn location services off!"
"But it will tell us if there are problems up-"
"Dad, seriously. We know how to get to the fucking cabin. You know I basically went AWOL right?"
"Can't you just email them? They can't penalise you for protecting yourself." Nimh is silent and bites her lip.
Rohan's brow is furrowed. "I don't know what the problem is?"
"Dad, turn location off. Shit, did you put the address in?"
"No, just Ruthglen."

Nimh sighs. "Okay, okay. Whatever." Nimh is irritated but too motivated to get to the destination to dwell on it.

"It's probably better that they know where you are anyway." Nimh growls through gritted teeth. "Dad." Rebuffed, Rohan falls silent.

"I still owe three months compulsory service. Obviously now would be a pretty optimum time to do it." Nimh focuses on the road ahead.

"I'm not underestimating how special you are darling but I don't think they're going to send a brigade to get you up here."

"They've got defence units at every port. If they know I'm in the Highlands, they could get someone to harass us from... Mallaig I guess. And by harass I mean..."

A long moment passes while the reality of the future settles over the car like ice. As they continue on the lone roads, Nimh tries the radio. It is laced with static but an occasional sentence gets through.

ON THE RADIO

- flared again in - - - as angry mobs of - - - retaliate - - - burned alive and homes des - - - avoid metropolit - - -travel at - - - disease accelerates in young ----

Rohan bristles and switches the radio, finding a classical station: a fiddle plays. He leans back, huge bags under his eyes. Skin pale. Eyes half closed with exhaustion. "I'm glad we're going to the cabin. It makes sense. It was the first place I truly lived, and it'll be the last."

Nimh looks over in protest but he has sunk back sleepily, his head nodding against his shoulder.

Nimh glances at Rohan, fast asleep like a child in the passenger seat. She has turned off the motorway and is driving smoothly through smaller village roads. They are in the Highlands, and it appears deserted.

Old stone walls bifurcate rolling fields which in turn give way to mountainous peaks. Ancient trees and small, white-washed houses dot the scenery. Nimh's eyes are strained, bloodshot. Her skin hollow with dehydration and fatigue. Rohan has been asleep for hours and she is glad that at least he will be rested. The long drive is starting to wear her down, not least because they are so near the cabin, the extra miles excruciating... Nimh confident in the fact that so far it looks safe, if empty. At the last turnoff before a one-way dirt road leads into the mountains, Nimh slows down as she passes a stone cottage on the side of the road.

Finally, a person. A middle aged man sits on a metal chair in the front door. It is cold but he is curiously not rugged up, sitting there in a thin woollen jumper and jeans. He stares out, vacant-eyes cast downward, arms crossed. Nimh wonders whether he's been on a watch and has fallen asleep, although the air is brisk. Out the corner of Nimh's eyes she thinks she sees a streak of blood and a pair of feet clad in low heeled shoes in the corridor - but it is dark and the car is moving too fast - no time to confirm what she might have seen. She slows down, looking in all mirrors, and just before making the turn off, sees several tyre tracks on the Man's property at a gateway to a large field. She stops the car and looks back - mud tracks circle outside the cottage. She turns around, leans back and grabs a hammer and knife; placing the knife in her lap she locks the doors and pulls back up to the Man's house. At close range, she sees his zip is undone, his mouth frozen in a semi-smile. His gums are black. Dead. Reversing back to the turn off, Nimh looks up the road, turns off the engine and opens the windows. She listens. The roar of engines combines with yelling and periodic screams, piercing the landscape.

Putting the windows up again, Nimh looks to her sleeping father. Dreading having to wake him.

She moves off, working off a theory. Backtracking to the next set of houses, she notices the mud tracks and a smashed window. No one appears to be there, no cars, no lights. As she considers the scene, the sound of a motorcade fills the air. Panic rising, she looks around, not sure if she's imagining it. She looks in the rear-view mirror, it's hard to be certain but a flicker appears on the horizon. Cars.

Nimh peels away back to the main road and nudges Rohan. "Dad, wake up."
Rohan slowly wakes up, disoriented and weak. "Dad, we're at Straithairn, leaving the cabin."
He rubs his eyes, not really taking in what she says. Nimh speaks softly but her heart is racing and her pupils wildly dilated. "How do we get to Mallaig?"
She reaches for some juice behind her seat, passes it to him.

He gratefully receives it and takes a swig.

"Dad, c'mon, think, which way to Mallaig right now? I need to turn - now!"

Struggling to focus his eyes on the road ahead, Rohan wakes himself up. "Uh, right. Go right. Then turn left at the farmhouse, then right."

"Are there any bigger roads?"

"What's going on?"

In the rear-view mirror, Nimh can see a band of cars moving toward them.

"The cabin was overrun. We need to get to get to a defence unit, Mallaig. But we can't get trapped in a one-way road system barricaded by stone walls."

Rohan fumbles for the phone, turning to the rear to see the approaching cars gunning towards them. "I...I know that...um, if we turn left, I just know the more scenic..." "Dad, focus - think. Put the phone away, we don't know if they're linked in or who can see it too. C'mon, pull it together. How do we get to a main road?"

Nimh navigates the thin roads, twisting and turning like a labyrinth in a Tudor garden, bound by impenetrable, ancient stone walls at least 4ft high.

"Okay, uh, at the end of this road go right - no - left to Oldhamstocks, we go through that village - it's two lanes - and then right over the bridge takes us to the motorway." Nimh turns left as directed but the road narrows to two farm properties. She panics and spins the car into a three point turn as quickly as possible. Mud and dirt fly off the wheels as the car jolts backwards and forwards. Straining to see the oncoming convoy, Nimh burns down the road to make the turn. The cars are less than 200m away and have started a sustained honking; the combined noises an industrial battle cry.

"Fuck!"

Rohan is tremulous, utter dread on his face. "Switch seats with me, hide under the blanket and I'll approach them, put them off - - -"

Pushing into full throttle precision driving mode, Nimh doesn't even hear him. "Direction, now!"

"Left!"

The car turns fluidly and powerfully around sharp country bends, over cattle grids and a narrow bridge. The cars have stopped honking in order to keep up, their cars bouncing and grazing the walls and roadways, the drivers reckless and hell bent on their quarry. Nimh and Rohan work in unison navigating and steering through the maze of Scottish villages until the road widens on approach to a large T intersection. "Right at the intersection."

Ploughing forward, Nimh takes the car to the motorway with a sharp right, without stopping. Once on the motorway, Nimh takes the car to an easy 140km per hour. The car breezes. Rohan looks back and sees the cars stalling at the intersection. Terrified but exhilarated, Rohan and Nimh grin with ashen faces.

Rohan's hand is gripped on the side handle, Nimh shakes off the adrenaline, exhilarated. "If we make it to Mallaig, we need to raise a serious fucking toast to Alan."

The car passes through miles of sparse, purple scenery. As they reach the outskirts of a small rural town, Nimh slows down.

Rohan peers ahead, he has binoculars in his hands.
"It looks empty."
Nimh is wary of a repeat of the morning's chase. "Does this road definitely open up?" Rohan answers cautiously, "I think so."
Nimh proceeds carefully. As they get closer, a couple of cars are parked discreetly at the side of houses. As they approach, Nimh sees a boy in between a couple of the houses, he's pouring water from a bucket into a dog bowl outside. His blue eyes are luminous under an unruly thatch of light ginger hair, his clothes well worn and starting to get raggedy, though he is dirty and his eyes are haunted. Arthur. His eyes hold Nimh's for a second before a figure appears at the door, an old man with hair the colour of faded wheat. Both look like their circumstances have been terribly reduced, clothes clean but in poor condition.
"Arthur, come in!"
Noticing Nimh he briefly puts his hands up, before pulling Arthur inside.
"Hey, wait!" Nimh jumps out the car despite Rohan's protestations. Three knocks on the old wooden door. Rohan has left the car and hurried to join Nimh; the sight of him

brings a few other men and boys out of the houses.
Arthur's Grandfather approaches, his feet clad in battered
Wellington boots, his footfall assured, stoic.

"I'm sorry, but we're full here."

Nimh steps forward. "What do you mean full?"

A sinewy man from an adjacent plot. steps forward to silence
the Grandfather.

Jim Muirfield is in his 70s, slight but with a strong
authoritative presence.

"We're a No Threat Zone. We don't want no trouble. But if
you're here asking for him," he gestures to Rohan, "he can
stay but you've got to move on."

Nimh responds, "I just wanted to know if there are any safe
villages left."

"We couldn't get near our place in Ruthglen" proffers Rohan.

The Grandfather and Jim Muirfield stand very still, until the
Grandfather nods.

"Aye.

"Do you have women here?" Nimh looks around, the houses
are tightly shut.

Jim takes the lead, his voice low and calm.

"No. Only us old men."

Nimh looks at the boy, Arthur, peering out from behind the
door.

"Where are your women?"

Jim stiffens, his bearing every inch a defiant Scot.

"For their safety, I will respectfully decline answering your
question."

"Okay. Can you tell us if Mallaig still stands? Is is defended?"

The Grandfather pipes up. "It stands."

"Okay, thank you." Nimh turns to leave, Rohan thanks the men, "Good luck to you." The men murmur good byes as Nimh and Rohan head back to the car.

Rohan sidles up to Nimh walking at a fast clip. "So we go to Mallaig."

She strides ahead, frustrated. "They could've been more helpful."

They get back in the car and start the engine. As they move off, Nimh catches something in the corner of her eye. Arthur is waving at her out the window, his small

serious face broken into a smile beneath his unruly hair. Nimh smiles and waves back at him, before his Grandfather whisks him away, closing the curtains.

Ascending the country road, the village grows smaller and smaller in the distance. Nimh is contemplating the strange set up, the quiet dignity of the old men and their chivalric organisation of their order. But also how they seemed...ill at ease, scared. Her ruminations are abruptly halted when a cavalcade of unmarked vehicles move toward them at speed.

"Shit. Dad, get down."

Rohan scrabbles in the back and gets under the blanket.

As the motorcade draws near the front car pulls up. The X-CELLE Unit is armed, and the driver has a gun levelled at Nimh's driver seat. Nimh has her card at the ready and puts the window down. The driver of the van, 2nd Lt Halsey has tightly scraped back hair and a severe expression which is only slightly softened by the sight of Nimh. Nimh pre-empts the conversation, adopting a confident and crisp voice. "Hi -

Nimh Singh. Formerly of Sussex 5, I am heading to Mallaig to defend the port." She scans the unreadable face of the driver. "We had family property here."

The driver immediately relaxes and changes her glance from squinting at Nimh's card to studying her face.

After a tense minute of staring, Halsey speaks in a flat voice. "Right. Don't go through the sea lochs. Stick to the A294. And get there as fast as possible. Are you logged in?" "Yes, but the signal was dropping - I nearly got caught up in a situation outside Ruthglen. A mob maybe 15 strong. "

2nd Lt Hasley's face tightens. "You didn't come up on our contacts."

Nimh deflects with total confidence. "Yeah the signal, and, I'm low battery - been driving for 12 hours or more. Just trying to get to Mallaig as fast as I can."

"Right. Steer clear of the sealochs."

"Thanks. Are you heading east?"

2nd Lt Hasley looks to the hill.
"No. We're heading there."

Nimh is disturbed but smiles broadly, "Oh, I just came through - it was cool, No Threat Zone."

The 2nd Lt gives her a strange look which Nimh can't quite decipher. She raises her hand and signals off. Nimh waits for the convoy to pass before moving off slowly. Scanning the horizon, it is clear.

"You alright Dad?"

Rohan comes out of his hiding place. "All that teenage dissembling has actually served a purpose. You're quite the actress."

Nimh shrugs. "I sensed a jobsworth."

As Rohan climbs in the front, Nimh keeps her eyes on the rear-view mirror. Three black crows swoop behind the car. The car crests the top of the hill, the village no longer in sight. Nimh pulls over.

"What are you doing?"

Nimh looks in the rearview mirror. "Just give me a sec."

Jumping out she grabs a knife out the back as a precaution and the pair of binoculars lifted from Alan's house. Moving to the top of the hill, she veers behind a tree. She can see the vans approach the village. She watches keenly, making sure she is obscured behind a long branch. Through the binoculars she can see the Unit methodically leave their vehicles. They are striding. Nimh cranes to see clearly. Within seconds sporadic gunfire perforates the atmosphere as Nimh sees the Unit descend upon the houses, despite the gunfire they are advancing with what look like bayonets. Nimh freezes, the colour draining from her face. Through the lens, she can see a thin man being dragged onto the side of the road in front of the houses. It is the Grandfather. A young boy suddenly darts out of the house, his movement a blur until a thickset soldier hooks an arm around him and slits his throat. In the slowed motion of the boy falling, she sees the boy's small shoulders, his flame coloured hair. Nimh drops the binoculars, immobilized by the horror of what is happening. Backing off, she starts to run to the car, jumping in and starting the engine.

"What was that?"

"Nothing, nothing. Let's go. But...go and lie down in the back. Just in case."

"I don't think that's necessary-"

"For me Dad." Nimh covers quickly. "If we get stopped by a Unit again they might think I'm deserting if they see you in the car."

Rohan grumbles but sees the logic in this. Nimh tries not to shake as she speeds down the road.

A young woman with bloodshot eyes, behooded, exhausted. Waiting in traffic, waiting with no sensation in her fingers.

A radio tuned to a local emergency frequency, the voice not matching the locale. RADIO V/O

Females are advised to stay indoors out of sight and dial the emergency number 333 at first sign of raiders. Do not call the police as traditional emergency services cannot be guaranteed. All cars will be searched on entry to Mallaig. Females are advised-

Bloodshot eyes hunt a place to park. Colourful houses arc around a deep port. Resident seagulls wait in glee. Hands off the wheel at last. They lie limp in her lap, fingers cramped into position.

Deep dark eyes, the smell of Old Spice on a starched shirt, a hug for a long beat. Whispered jubilation: "You were brilliant. Just brilliant."

Breathing him in, eyes scrunched up to soak in the moment.

Nimh and Rohan wait in the small reception of a Bed &
Breakfast. Rohan sits in a chair, waiting, exhausted with a
pounding head. Nimh stands at a wooden desk, a little
Highland Bull made with red and yellow tartan stares at her
from the guest book. A plump woman is writing in a sign-in
book, she is under pressure and has a disapproving air.
"You can have the one night, but we're fully booked
tomorrow. Provided you have cash."
"We do. People are making bookings online right now?"
The receptionist, who is also the Landlady, tilts her chin at a
supercilious angle.
"No, locals are booking." Nimh feels the familiar distance,
used to brokering the space between acceptance and
alienation.
"We're from near here. My mother w- is Scottish. Our place
got overrun at Ruthglen." The Landlady is clearly surprised
and not tactful enough to hide it. "Well then, you should know
we've actually got a Unit coming, three defenders apparently.
But of course, you've already heard there's been trouble."

"Yeah, I'll bet a fair few people are heading here. Safety in
numbers."
The Landlady purses her lips while she registers more
information on the computer. "Aye, well you have a good
night's sleep and see me about the room in the morning. "
Nimh takes the keys that rest on the counter, they are
attached to a plastic disc with a map of the Isle of Skye.
"Thanks."
Nimh swings her backpack over her shoulder, catching the

Landlady looking coldly at Rohan.

"That your husband dear?"

"No. It's my Dad."

"Aye, ooh I'm sorry. You just never know these days, didn't mean to offend. And I'm sorry to ask, but how... advanced is he?"

The question cuts Nimh to the bone. The intoxicating closeness of a private, warm room, a soft bed, a cup of tea and the pre-emption of safety shattered by this intrusion of reality. She looks the woman in the eye.

"He has a headache, not the disease." She conspiratorially pulls out an X-Celle card, holding it in front of the woman. "You've heard of the 1% ers? I work for the genetic coding program. My father is it's most experienced sequencer."

The plump woman trembles, suddenly obsequious. "Oh, dear, well you let me know if there's anything you need..."

Nimh seizes the moment. "We've had a long and dangerous drive... Is there anywhere to get food?"

"Of course you poor thing - I'll bring a wee supper up to your room."

"That's kind of you, thanks." Nimh smiles sweetly without losing the stature and superiority the lie has afforded her. "Oh, and we'll need the room for a month. We can pay cash."

"Yes, yes, of course!"

Nimh turns away, suppressing a desire to roll her eyes. She picks up Rohan's bag, almost sinking under the weight, and pulls him by the elbow.

"C'mon Dad. You've got a lot of top secret genetic sequencing to do tomorrow." Nimh smiles at the gleaming eyed Landlady and helps her Dad upstairs.

Nimh is fast asleep, her face peaceful, lost in deep dreams.

Sitting in the bed opposite her, Rohan looks down on his daughter. His eyes brim, an endless well of love. Nimh stirs and rolls over, gripping the blankets tight. Rohan give a small smile and goes to the window, the room overlooks the port, it arcs around around the ancient coastline, lined with tall terraces built to withstand the onslaught of rain storms and freezing winters. A beautiful sunrise spreads light over the harbour, making the lines of colourful houses glow like a rainbow.

Rohan takes the unexpected view in, allowing the morning sun to bathe his face. He takes its full measure, feeling its restorative energy. As his chin returns to rest down on his chest, he notices his forearms, stretched out to rest his hands on the window sill.

The spots which were a faint grey have deepened in colour, and started to merge. The sight chills him, a lurch of panic hitting his stomach. He closes his eyes for a long beat, then looks at the rising sun once again.

"Ah, Sleep of the Gods!" Nimh is awake, luxuriating in the bliss of a good night's sleep. "Did you sleep?"
Rohan takes a deep breath and turns to her, face tranquil,

any hint of foreboding gone. "Like a log." His face brightens. "How about we go and get some breakfast?"

Nimh yawns in agreement. "Perfect."
"The landlady does the best porridge on the mainland according to Expedia. We have until 9am to put it to the test."
"What time is it?"
"Just gone 8. We have time."
"Great. Oh, dad? Um, I think I told her you were a genetic scientist and were...um...immune."
"Why would you say that?"
Nimh buries her head in the pillow. "Arrrgh. Because she was about to throw us out... Dad, I was barely lucid last night."
Rohan considers, folding a scarf in his hands to take downstairs. "Genetic scientist. Like you, eh?"
"Yes, but with actual qualifications and a long career behind you."
Rohan gets a leather book from his bag and heads to the door. "See you down there, I'll be solving Rubix Cubes and brushing up on some quantum physics while I wait. You know, the usual."

Nimh throws him a look as she gets out of bed.

A tartan-carpeted breakfast room with formica topped tables, photographs sealed behind aged shadow boxes. A small buffet is set up underneath a counter window.

Each of the dozen or so tables is filling up fast; almost all with women and girls although male family members dot the room too. The atmosphere is surreal in its normalcy: Someone complains that the milk needs to be topped up, steaming pots of tea are brought to tables.

Nimh notices Rohan has already settled in with a plate of toast and scrambled eggs. She gets herself a bowl of porridge and sits at the table, pulling her chair so she is in view of the road outside. "Not willing to test y'olde Expedia this fine morn?"

Rohan smiles. "Not sure I've quite the stomach for it today."

Nimh sees his stoicism and realises he has barely touched his eggs, just nibbled a few pieces of toast. His shirt sleeves are buttoned tight around his wrists. Anxiety floods her face. She lowers her voice. "Show me your arms."
Rohan stays focused on the murmur of activity outside.

"Dad..."
"Not here Nimmy."

They sit in silence. Nimh can feel her heart race and hands go numb. Neither one touching their plates. The breakfast server, a middle aged woman with an apron, looks fixedly at their table.

Nimh feels the stare and takes a sip of juice.

The breakfasters startle as a crash sounds in the distance; scattered screams and commotion rumble outside. The serving woman moves to the window as breakfasters shift in their seats, caught between fearful curiosity and hunger.

Nimh jumps up and cranes her neck out the window. A few people hurry past the window but the mood is of caution rather than panic.

Nimh goes back to the table, jugs the rest of the orange juice. "I'm going to go and see what's up...Try and eat something Dad."

Rohan smiles and raises his cup of tea. Willing himself to let her go without suffocating her with worry, pleading with his eyes for her to use caution.

Nimh slips out.

Nimh walks briskly down the street, clocking everything around her. People are starting to peep out of doors and a few walk around with shopping bags and laundry. War zone life. Immediate threat dismissed, life continues as normal until the next crash, the next scream, the next crush. A thin a spire of black smoke curls toward the sky on the outskirts of the small town. The terraced houses have slim gaps where cobbled alleys snake their way to the bigger roads circling the town. A small crowd has gathered on the periphery of one of the broadest alleys that leads to one of the main arteries into the port. Over shoulders and hat or hoodie covered heads, Nimh catches a glimpse of black-clad figures sweeping the scene. The familiar sight of an X-Celle Defense Unit.

Nimh pushes through the crowd and sees a four-wheel drive and two sedans crashed with considerable force into a house above the alley. One of the cars is spun on its side, having dissected a stone wall, another is crumpled against a front window, it's bonnet folded up to the back seats like a concertina. Nimh immediately counts three male bodies on the ground. If they didn't die of their injuries, they were most certainly shot. A tall and athletic soldier is calmly and efficiently erecting a barrier around the crash. She has an open, calm face and appears to be in her late twenties. On seeing Nimh approach her, she pauses.

"Please stand back." Notices her youth, the soldier changes tone, "Are you carded to be here?" She reads Nimh's indecision. "You should be with Mallaig D-1, they're at the town hall. It's a HURRICANE alert."

Nimh takes that in, and also the soldier's generous mouth, soft eyes and honest face. "I, I just came up from Sussex 5." Enunciating with meaning. "Me and my Dad."

Rose reads what's going on and sees Nimh's conflicted face. She moves aside and talks quietly, cordon tape in hand. "I'm sure that you understand that Hurricane evokes martial law. Not that I'm suggesting you are a deserter, because you obviously came up here to register where the fight needed you most."
"Yes. Absolutely. I came to fight...and see how long this town has left."
"Show me your card."
Nimh slowly turns it over. Rose looks at it closely, then pulls out her phone and scans it.
"Please don't-"

The phone beeps.

"It's set to search. Don't panic...Turn your phone on. And check into Highlands. Highlands X. Sooner rather than later."

"I thought you said Delta 1?"

"Yeah."

"I haven't heard of Highlands X."

Rose gives an implacable stare, Nimh notices a grey badge underneath an epaulet: two swords crossed in an X. "How bad are the gangs? Will the port make it?"

"Turn on your phone. Go to Highland X. Do it by midday."

"How? They don't even know me?"

"The system will accept your score."

"When did grouping become automatic?"

Rose snaps the tape and starts to walk back to the armoured vehicle. She gives a final look to Nimh. "You can die with your Dad, badly, or you can survive fighting."

Rose starts to move off, into the fray, calling one last time over her shoulder. "Turn on your phone!"

Conflict gnaws at Nimh as she stands on the scene. She takes the three limp bodies lying on the ground, the twisted car-cans hurtled like bullets into residential houses, the pale faces of the villagers standing around in shock, the lithe professionalism of Rose, and most terrifying of all, her warning, her advice, her command.

As the surreal vista swirls in front of Nimh, an old farm car approaches down the road, swaying from side to side. The paramilitary group moves into a defensive alignment and signals for the car to stop. The vehicle keeps going for a few seconds and then veers to a shaky halt. A few tense beats before a door swings open. The soldiers pace toward the car, guns drawn. Suddenly, a very thin man appears, using all his strength to pull something out of the seat. Two of the soldiers approach the car, guns drawn, warning him to stop. The man is either possessed or catatonic and doesn't appear to hear them. Guns are levelled when the man finally frees something from the car, a young teenage girl, nearly naked with only a torn camisole and bloodied underpants on. Blood from her mouth runs in a rivulet down her frozen face. Streaming down her legs, blood coursing over what looks like caked on viscera.

The man holds her up as they stumble to the unit; the young girl keels forward, eyes at once vacant and wild. Hair plastered around her face like a feral animal. The soldiers seize her arms and raise an alarm, "CASEVAC!"

The two look like they have been in a war zone. The man appears to be a grandfather, or perhaps a father, her father, withered by disease. As the Unit medics swirl around the girl, he collapses.

Nimh has instinctively entered the scene and darted forward to the two badly injured; she pauses as the Unit almost effortlessly shifts its choreography from potential conflict scenario to medical evacuation, lifting the girl and carrying her to a van as the scene is cleared. Shouts of 'MEDIC' and the horrified gasps on onlookers slow down around Nimh's ears. She sees the old man lying in the road, no one attends to him

in the desperate seconds of trying to save the girl. Nimh runs
to him.

Lying on his side, his eyes almost closed, he breathes raspily.
His arms are almost black. Nimh takes hold of his hand, lifts
his head onto her lap. "She's going to be okay, she's going to
be okay."
Her words evaporate. Nimh holds the man, the wind knocked
out of her chest. She sits there as time stands still. She holds
his lifeless body tight, rocking slightly. She is lost to the
rythym of the desolate scene when a shadow crosses over
her. It is Rose,

standing above, her calm and implacable face watching Nimh
immersed in tragedy, splashed with blood.
"Were you issued a weapon?"
"No."

"Highland X will issue you one." She looks down at Nimh
holding the strange man, a kindred softness in her eye.
"We're a raid division. We stop shit like this before it gets to
town."
"I'm not a 1%er."

"Yeah, you are."
That catches Nimh's attention.
"There's a unit leaving at dusk and dawn. I'll be on the dawn."
Nimh reels. "Wait - is it true that 1%ers can get... medicine?"
Rose holds her attention for moment and then smiles. "See
you there."Nimh takes in the smile.
As Rose walks away, on mission, Nimh moves the man's head,

crouches down and lifts his emaciated frame onto her
shoulder. He's still very heavy. She staggers to a nearby
house and calls out. "Can I get some help?"

A woman standing in a garden near the crash comes forward,
helps to hold the man. They lower him onto the ground in the
front garden. The Villagewoman lowers him gently to the
grass, "Easy does it."
People are milling about everywhere in the aftermath of the
commotion. Carts are already taking the crash-attackers
away as a thickset Officer makes her way to Nimh. Nimh
doesn't notice, looks to the Villagewoman.

"Thanks. Do you mind-- do you have a pen and paper? To ID
him-"
"Oh, good call. Hard to believe it's come to this. Hang on."
The Villagewoman disappears into the house as Nimh kneels
by the man. She rolls down his sleeves, his face etched in
pain, regret. It shakes Nimh to the core. She waits with him,
looking up as the Villagewoman brings out a pen and a piece
of paper she has torn out of a notebook in her hand. It has
writing on it already, she passes it to Nimh.
"Here, I put the time and the incident with the girl, I'll go and
grab the car reg. If it has one."
"Cool. Good thinking."
As the Villagewoman leaves with the notebook, Nimh stares
at the woman's writing. She turns the page over and scrawls
on it, attaching it to the man's front pocket. Without her
noticing, the Officer has approached, a sturdy woman in her
30s. "We'll take it from here."

Nimh looks up at the Officer. "Don't put him in with the others. He was a civilian."

"I know. He'll be logged and taken care of."

Nimh pauses, giving him a last look before springing up. She thanks the Oficcer and doesn't look back as she moves to the alleys.

In the mild breeze of the overcast morning, the top of a piece of paper sticks out of a dead man's pocket. Scrawled in thick black letters a solitary word: "HERO."

A strong cold wind reverberates through the wind-tunnel alleys that lead back to the town. Nimh feet running quickly, her black trainers splashing through shallow puddles in the cobbled stone. At the end of the alley is an damp stone building, she stops in front of it, placing her hand on its textured surface, trying to let it's ancient energy slow her racing heart.

After a moment, she pulls out her phone. Stares at it for a second, then turns it on. A pulsating, radiating red circle glows as it comes alive. A bleating rhythm of messages and alerts comes through, she bypasses them and goes straight to a check-in page. Location turned on, she selects Mallaig. The phone instantly diverts her to an icon: Highland X. She clicks on it. The phone flashes up: RECEIVED.

Nimh walks back to the hotel, winding through the streets until she reaches the familiar façade the B & B. The streets are calm and she takes a moment to appreciate the hotel's traditionally Scottish, unassuming charm, this place that have given them safe harbour. The phone beeps continuously, breaking her reverie. It is a call, the number withheld. "Hello?"Nimh stands up straight, listening, then looking around. "Of course. No, not really, I'm...yes, sorry, the bookshop? Yes, red door, thanks." Nimh hurriedly walks across the street and into the market square. Rows of local produce and wool shops take pride of place in the square, but at the corner is a second hand bookshop with a selection of new releases out the front.

Nimh slows down and enters the book-shop, going to a book-stand at the entrance and taking a quick look. She then makes her way in slowly, as though browsing. A radio plays over the rows of books:

RADIO NEWS (V.O.)

A rogue jet fighter has dived into the women's college at the University of Cambridge in the latest episode which has prompted talks to disband the military. Wielding massive power in the hands of an armed force of predominantly male -

A Bookseller watches Nimh with shrewd eyes. As Nimh holds up a book with a red cover the woman gives an imperceptible nod and glances to the back. Nimh acknowledges the glance. At the back, there is a small corridor, to the left a stairwell lined with boxes of old paperbacks. A red door lies at the bottom of the stairs.

Nimh walks down the spiralling stone steps, adroitly evading the tripwire books. She gives a slight knock in a specific pattern before opening the door cautiously.

Inside the cement basement is a small living room - it could be plucked from a retirement village save for the fact that there are no windows and the wall is lined with computers and routers. A decorative jug and flowers sit on a coffee table. Jill, a serious-faced woman in her 50s, turns from the computer desk and comes forward.

"Hello, I'm Jill Ashcroft. Nice to meet you."

"Hi, Nimh Singh, you too."
Jill gestures to the settee. "Take a seat."
As Nimh sits, Jill brings over an electronic tablet and some notebooks. "So you're joining us from all the way down south."
"Yeah, I..."
"I'm not looking for an explanation. We anticipate volatility in this phase."
"You mean the gangs?"
"No, I mean amongst our own."
Nimh looks abashed.
"Grief is a many headed beast. We will all lose many who we love dearly. Not many keep a straight head in its midst." Jill looks to her notes.
"Our street was besieged. We have property here.. my Dad had nothing to do with it. He's an incredible human being... He brought me up after my mother..."
"You don't have to explain. We are in a different scenario now,

and you're part of Highland X. So let's focus on that."

A silence descends while Jill clicks her tablet shut. Nimh grabs the moment.

"Is it...sorry if this is impertinent to ask, or if this is just a rumour...but do 1%ers really have...um, access..."

"To a cure?" Nimh looks up at her, eyes wide and terrified of her response either way. "There's no cure."

Nimh's cheeks burn.

"But there is treatment. It is something that can be managed."

Nimh's eyes widen.

"It's not free. And it's not for everyone."

Nimh looks stricken.

"How much is it?"

"It depends what you're prepared to give. In service."

"I'll do anything."

"There is a treatment facility in Glasgow. It is possible, if not probable, that your father would be able to apply for a round of what we call 'Push-Back.' But I need to assign you a rank before we can start discussing benefits."

"Yes, sorry, yes."

"You were an excellent student. You are on a path to become a genetic sequencer. Is that what you want to do?"

"I love science. Yeah, or something related."

"You topped academic scores in three counties. But you're a lazy student, apparently. Though that's often a question of stimulation. Were you over or under? It looks like you enjoyed extra-curricular stimulation which may have detracted from your work." Nimh is shocked at the level of information she has. "Possibly, although if I topped the county perhaps it was the appropriate balance."

"Do you remember your history modules?"

"Yes?"

"Okay. It's like this. We have a platoon of X-Celle soldiers assembled to take on an increasingly virulent form of attack. We need smart people with weapons training." "I didn't do the finals..."

"I know. You're fast, you can shoot, and you're young. But you're also smart. I wouldn't normally put someone of your capabilities in a theater of combat but, frankly, we're at Hurricane."

"I heard."

"Do you know why?"

"Not exactly but guessing it's the vigilante gangs."

"Vigilante? Do you think there's an element of justice or extenuation in these attacks?"

"Well, legions of men are about to have their lives taken away without their consent" "And you think that murdering and torturing innocents, which is what has led to this Corrective Measure, is a justifiable response?"

Nimh shifts in her seat, backing away from an unwinnable argument.

"No, of course not."

Jill surveys her carefully. When she speaks, she enunciates very clearly. "Einsatzgruppen." "Your record says you did sit in on this module, were you paying attention?"

Nimh takes in this volley of questions, a line that seems to be constantly changing tack.

"What does it mean?"

"Pilling Kits (flustered) I mean, Killing Pits. Nazis swept through shooting civilians into mass graves they made them dig."

"Yes, although there were many different methods. Do you remember what the word means, Einsatzgruppen?"

"Something... group..."

"Action Groups."

There is an uncomfortable beat while Nimh calculates what Jill is getting at.

"Are you telling me we are going to be... Highland X is a... mobile killing squad?" Jill laughs. "Oh god no." Adding dryly, "We're the remedy, not the problem." She looks at Nimh intensely. You came all the way up from... Sussex... when?"

"I think we left three days ago."

"Ah. You missed The Fall."

Nimh waits for her to continue.

"The Gangs. Some are literally death throes, sporadic, violent, random or, targeted toward family members, revenge attacks on former lovers, unrequited lovers... the usual when women are murdered. But something else has mutated rapidly as the pathogen seems to have slowed, giving more time for men to take action."

"It's slowed?" Nimh's eyes flash.

"In certain men, yes. Usually just the young, and robust." Jill registers Nimh's disappointment. "Coordinated squadrons of men are leaving metropolitan areas and targeting small towns. Many are armed, many are not sick, yet." Jill gets up and goes to one of the computer screens. It is a map of the UK with images.

"A man called John Son has mobilized gangs of more than 50 men at a time sweeping from village to village. He's very quickly organised regions into cells."

The map is scarred with red bands. Nimh looks horrified.

"If we just take a look here... Highlands. This band is moving in. John Son is personally leading it."

"Why is he here and not somewhere, more strategically significant?"

A thick arc of red is closing in around Mallaig. Jill casually deflects, "We're a port and a gateway. There's strategy in that."

"Who is he?"

"Look for yourself."

Jill passes Nimh a print out of a photo and bio of John Son. He looks like a crass hedge funder.

"John Son, also known as Darren Craiglea, is an investment banker with a penchant for acquiring ski resorts and media entities. He' driven a news campaign claiming that the disease is being transmitted by women, so if you clear villages of women, presumably you can safeguard the men. They are working their way from remote regions into the more heavily defended metropolitan zones. Amassing an army."

"Is it true, do we carry the pathogen?"

"Of course not. But it's a clever and insidious piece of disinformation."

Nimh takes this in.

"As I said, we would prefer for you to have your nose in a lab or in a book."

Nimh looks very disturbed.

"What are you feeling?"

"Nothing, it's obviously a shock. I thought the north would be... Empty actually." "Would you like a cup of tea?"

"No, thanks. What do I need to do now?"

"I recommend a rank and you will be assigned to a platoon in Highland X. Though I have concerns."

Nimh looks up, alarmed.

"You said "Pilling Kits." Want to talk about that?"

Nimh realises she is fighting for her right to be a 1%er, the only chance she has of helping Rohan.

"Sorry, it's nothing."

"It's actually a sign of trauma."

"Our lecturer - you can look him up - Dr Konrad Swiet - was a child in the Holocaust, in the camps. Unbelievable intellect, spoke six languages fluently. But couldn't ever say killing pit. It was funny for a second, and then very, very... not funny."

The explanation seems to satisfy Jill.

"What are John Son's men calling themselves?"

"How do you know they are?"

"You said they were organised. Coordinated."

"Reaktiongruppen."

Rohan writes in his diary. Very weak, his face strained. Nimh opens the door and moves straight toward the bathroom.

She washes her hands thoroughly. Glancing up to the mirror she notices her face, speckled with dried blood, it is also on her jumper.

"What's going on? Are you okay?" "All good Dad. Hang on."

Nimh exits the bathroom, face damp but clean. She makes her way straight to Rohan, folds her arms around him. He strokes her hair.

"Is it that bad?"

She releases him and sits on her bed.

"Maybe."

"Was it a gang?"

The thought of the dead marauders, the sickening injuries of the girl and her poor grandfather flash through her mind..

"Nimh?"

Childish insouciance and deflection gone.

"Yeah, it's getting bad. The good news is the Greys are taking hold much slower than expected. The bad news is the backlash is...bad."

"Is it coming here, to town?"

"A bit." Nimh twists a thread in the woollen blanket. "I logged in Dad. I joined a Unit."

"Okay... I'm proud of you."

"I'm still going to be here, I don't want to lose any time."

"It's okay darling, it...it makes me very relieved that you will find a place. Makes me very happy." Rohan glances at the suitcase of Alan's fine goods by the window. "Plus I've got all those books to go through."

Nimh attempts to smile.

"When do you start? I saw some groups at the Town Hall filling sand bags... they were very cheery. Even offered me tea."

"Did you have some?"

"They take it to a different level these Scots. So strong I could almost levitate. But very nice, I spoke to a lovely woman, Abigail was her name, Abigail from Aberdeen who was a uh, task force manager I think-"

"Dad, it worries me you were walking around without telling me"

"Darling, it was just across the road, I told the Lady at the desk-"

Nimh suddenly makes sense of the Landlady's "grey to the eyeballs" comment. "Abigail said that supplies and defences here are solid, most the work is in regulating the flow of people and keeping the community functioning during the transition- you know, kids at school and food supplies consis-"

"I'm not going to be at the Town Hall Dad."

Rohan stops in his tracks.

"You can't go back home. And London's overrun. They need help here."

"I'm going to be here Dad."

"I got... commandeered into Highland X."

"What's that? Nimh?" Nimh takes a deep breath.

"It's an attack division. They raid the raiders."

Rohan stares at her, disbelief flooding his face.

"That doesn't make any sense. None whatsoever."

Nimh stays silent, waiting for the shock to pass.

"Well they've put you in the wrong division. You need to tell them you have no experience- you're not cannon fodder, you're a scientist!"

"They know that Dad. They know my modules."

Rohan is completely distressed.

"I did do the weapons course. I just didn't do the finals because it was all military tactical... I just couldn't..."

"It doesn't matter what you did and didn't do. Your worth as a scientist and engineer outstrips the fact you completed some... weapons training."

Nimh looks him straight in the eye.

"Unless the threat is so severe that they need each and every one of us with training." A heavy silence fills the space between them.

"Tell me." Nimh averts his gaze. "I'm dead already Nimh, and I'm...okay. Tell me what is going on."

"Please Dad...Some of the attacks are informally grouped vigilantes, no-structure- blood-lust. But there are some, bigger, squads who have left their localities to attempt a more... traditional attack posture."

Rohan's face pales. "Go on."

"They're leaving metropolitan areas to wipe out smaller villages. They're calling themselves the Reaktiongruppen."

"Are they, German?"

"No. They're just losers."

"Why isn't the damn disease not working fast enough?"

"Dad, calm down"

Rohan is breathing heavily, he struggles to stand, accidentally swiping a glass of water off the side table.

"This was never on the cards - this level of – war"

"It's an uneven fight Dad. In our favour."

Rohan shakes his head, hands clasped tightly.

"Dad, please, sit down. We're armed, with training - they're sick"

"Good God Nimh! That's their advantage! Not yours! No fighter is as lethal as the one who knows they are already dead."

Nimh steadies him, gripping his arm. He yelps out in pain. "I'm sorry, I'm sorry - Dad, please sit. Listen to me. We have a colossal advantage." Rohan sinks down. "Why you?"

"My score that you were so worried about. I'm a 1%er now." Rohan looks up at her with a baleful stare.

A girl wanting normalcy desperately, wearing a rainbow coloured jumper in a sea of blacks and browns and neutral inoffensive offensive camouflage clothes. Her father, disease ricocheting through his muscle memory, spine slumping, a bright smile bursting through clammy perspiration. The radiance of the girl, his light, his salve. Wherever she is, the world turns.

A restaurant at the end of the world, a tiny sea port in the far flung isles of western Scotland, as busy as a Soho nightclub in the sweating season.

The night-time is for laughing, and pretending day won't come.

NIMH follows an icon in her phone through the streets, people seem relaxed and none of the women have their hoods up. She glances at a family of two girls walking arm in arm with both their parents, the father looks frail yet his embrace of them is protective. People stand outside coloured houses with cups of tea: the atmosphere is bright but cautious, a certain desensitization to the extreme circumstances that have shaped their world for months. Nimh leaves the chatter and activity of the streets and alleys, coming out towards moored boats. Rain starts to fall.

By the entrance to the docks, a lookout of men and women sit in a row on chairs with flasks of tea and whisky. They watch the horizon sharply as they chatter. As the rain deepens, they turn up the collars of their yellow mackintoshes.

Nimh walks quickly, passing colourful sheds and cheery boats toward older, more industrial vessels.

The icon on the phone flares. She looks around, there are a handful of old warehouse buildings wrapped in corrugated iron. She approaches one, iron rusting off it's corners, it's drains gush with rain water. She pulls to the side, huge rickety doors sealed shut. Still, she notices what look like small circles half concealed on the building's edges. Cameras. She stands outside the doors.

Abruptly, the door is pullied open. A familiar face stands before her, a youthful soldier with a kind face. Rose.

"Glad you could make it."

Nimh casts her eyes around the room. It is just a bare warehouse with mariner's supplies stacked in a corner. A table, chairs and a couple of whiteboards with maps and a small computer and radio console. Rose observes Nimh with amusement.

"Were you expecting M15 in here?"

"Well not the ancient mariner's sea shack." Rose smiles.

Rohan sits at table in the corner. It hasn't been cleared from the previous occupants so is crammed with glasses and scraped clean plates. There is one spare chair sitting opposite him.

A blonde woman enters the restaurant, her eyes scan the room for a spare seat.

Rohan waits patiently, opens his diary and thinks carefully before starting to write. A Server comes and hastily clears the table, Rohan lifts his diary out of the way.

The Blonde Woman spies the table being cleared off and approaches. She is tall, lean with an aristocratic bearing and intelligent eyes. When she speaks, her voice bears the soft glow of an Irish accent.

"Excuse me, sorry but is anyone sitting with you?"

Rohan is startled but not unpleasantly so. "My daughter will be joining me at 7.30..." "Ah, not to trouble you then."

"But you're welcome to sit until then."

"Are you sure? Thank you kindly. I won't disturb you."

Rohan adjusts his diary to rest at an angle on the table, giving her more room. "Hope you're not hungry. It takes them awhile to take orders."

"I heard they were serving hot food, I don't care how long I have to wait."

They share a conspiratorial laugh.

"I never thought I'd regret not watching all of those Hollywood dystopias my daughter was so mad about. I might have been better prepared for the tinned goods." "Then let's just hope order is restored soon, for the sake of epicurians everywhere." The moment is bittersweet, Rohan's eyes well. "Indeed, indeed."

Soldiers are milling around and one of them is fast-forwarding through footage on a computer. More young recruits, men and women, filter in until the place is packed. Only a handful have uniform. Nimh watches with interest.

"Are we all 1%ers now?"
Rose doesn't answer, busy talking to a new recruit.

Nimh peers over her shoulder to see graphic footage of women in the middle east, completely covered, chattel. One of them is yanked out and publicly stoned. Blurry images of men and boys watching the scene, frothing at the mouth in their enthusiasm.

Nimh looks to Rose. "What is this, Jihadis Just Wanna Have Fun?"
"Nah, that's...2014. Business as usual. "
The firm voice of a Commanding Officer booms across the room. "Assemble."

The group collect themselves before a huge map on a screen next to a whiteboard. "Grab a seat, sit while you can."
Nimh leans in to Rose, "I thought this was just a brief. Rose gives her a shrug.

"Welcome to our newest recruits, we appreciate you have all left other posts to join us here. Tonight's theme is this: Offense Lies at the Heart of Defense. Consider those words. Many of you will have noticed the marauding attacks on the population; boys gone wild."

A female Recruit with piercing eyes listens intently. "I've seen women too, Ma'am. Women participating in the attacks."

The CO looks directly at the outspoken recruit. Concealing irritation at being interrupted.

An irate younger man joins in. "What, were they raping children and grannies as well?"

"No. They were scalping breasts with a butcher's knife." A murmur ripples through the recruits.

"Our job is to protect innocents. It certainly won't be the first time in recent history misguided simpletons act against their own interests, but it will hopefully be the last."

"I saw vans with tubes... With gas in them."

The Commanding Officer turns to the board.
"That's not a new method. Radical change kills Radically. And so it has.And so it will. It is now in your hands who will survive to build the future. It is now in your hands how these murderers leave this earth. You decide. They can wither from disease and take your sisters and mothers and babies with them, or you can consign their violence to history and bring

freedom and safety to those who will build the planet's future."

The atmosphere is charged. The Recruits are silenced, and intensely focused. Nimh is altered. Her face serious, hands stock still in her lap.

Rohan takes the last sip from his glass of water. "I think if we don't order we might get kicked out."

"We could give it another ten minutes? It's only 8…" "Let's order. Was it hard getting out of Dublin?"

"Oh, I came up from London. I was working for a couple of weeks. I got out just before the barracks went berserk, women getting shot on the streets."
"Why Mallaig? Is this seriously the only safe outpost left?" Gwendoline gives Rohan a mysterious smile.

"No, there are plenty of others. Mallaig may not be as safe as you think." Rohan shifts in his seat.
"I figured air transport might be down so I'm catching a boat."
"To where?"

A rainbow coloured jumper trapped under a bullet proof vest..

If you see him, signal to one of us first, understand? Tap twice. Only shoot if there is no resort. Hold fire until the sig comes through.

I know, I know!

All the others wear combat boots, steel capped and ground by gravity, but she is light, an airbound misfit clad in old trainers.

Why don't I get boots?

So you can run.

Smoke and low light. Rohan is emotional and a little tipsy, his face pale and slightly sweaty. He doesn't look well but is clearly absorbed in a connection with Gwen. She listens deeply, leaning forward.
"She was a lucky soul. To have someone love her so."

"When we first married... I used to say, and think....Would give my life for her. Die for her! Romeo with stars in his eyes. But then came Nimh. And Marian and I... all our fire, it all went to her." Rohan's body sways in the din.
"You're a good father Rohan."

"I just wish... with my dying breath... How can I leave her like this?"
Gwendoline leans back, thoughts flooding her face. She glances first at her hands, then at Rohan. He is poorly and starting to look desperate.
Rohan grabs his watch from his shirt pocket, checks the time.
"It's been over four hours. Where is she?"
"Rohan, I may be able to help."

He doesn't hear, peering out the window, shuffling to get up. Gwendoline gently touches his upper arm.

The air prickles, moisture clamming hair but air too dry to breathe easily. A clamour of soldiers boots, anxiety bursting through straps and buckles. A young woman looking for an escape route.

"The boat leaves at 7am. From there it's a four hour drive, the refuge won't turn her away. I can vouch for her."

Rohan looks at her intensely, sweating through his brows. "How?"
"I helped originate the seed bank program; the refuge is built around it." "She'll never go."

Nimh sidles up to Rose.

"Hey, I thought this was just a briefing."

"It was. We got the brief."

"It's just that I left my Dad, I need to call him and tell him to lay low."

Rose sighs, glancing at the CO. "I don't know if you can."

"I'll just tell him I'm getting kitted out... He's too sick to stay out all night... and you said yourself, we're at Hurricane. He won't know about the curfew. Please."

Rose looks uncertain, her troubled gaze broken by the CO.

"There's been a large attack on the east coast. An amassed division is moving west. John Son has ordered advance attack units to converge: we expect movement within 8 hours, Mallaig could be a direct target."

The group shrinks at the enormity of the threat.
"Be thorough. Move fast."
Soldiers shuffle around and intensify their preparations.
Nimh looks to Rose. "Go. Hurry. One call. Don't let her see."
Nimh wastes no time

Nimh stands next to the door, facing out to the deserted dock, dotted with empty

vessels and long abandoned fishing gear. She starts to dial her father.

A surreal blur of high-pitched sound, smoke and destruction. Nimh gets up, disoriented and alone. Her head is bleeding, sight blurry. She looks out at the scene, dismembered bodies smoking in the ruins. Her head spins.

Darkest before the dawn, the town sleeps with one eye open. Past the glistening black of the port, Rohan leans on Gwendoline for support.

She packs the car as fast as she can with Rohan and Nimh's bags. The sound of gunfire taps in the distance.

Nimh runs with all her strength back to the B & B. Feet dragging through the air, feet she cannot feel.

Miraculously sure-footed on cobbled alleys which lead to the main street, she passes a Butcher's Shop with a long mirror facing the street. As she flashes by she catches a glimpse of a shadowy figure, streaked with red and brown and black.

Unrecognizable. Speckles of someone else's blood dot her face like obscene freckles. Disoriented but charged with adrenaline, she runs as chaos and panic begins to erupt all around.

Very weak, Rohan sits on the bed, breathing heavily. A key turns in the lock.

Relief turns to a hug that shatters time and sense and a pleading disconsolate sob, disorientation and splitting heads and bleeding lips and they are in the car. Fingers taking up a practised grip, eyes on the road ahead.

Nimh's head has stopped bleeding and apart from a few cosmetic scratches she looks okay. The chaos and violence is catching up to them as they make their way through the seaside town. It is a short drive away from the main port to a small jetty. Groups of people are starting to leave town, take their chances. Car doors are locked tight as stragglers try to jump in; an elderly woman is knocked down in the scrabble as cars start tearing away from the port.

"Is this it?"

Rohan looks ahead and catches a tall blonde figure in the distance. His long range sight is compromised.

"Is that the woman?"

"Gwendoline. Thank God."

Nimh looks at the clock.

"Dad, I've got to get to a Unit... you go with her and I'll meet up with you later-" Despite the plea, Nimh sounds unconvinced.

A large boat dwarfs the small jetty, guarded by a unit of heavily armed women. They are checking the id's of all the would be travellers and holding back those who are not on the list, a crush of panicked people desperately plead with the guards to allow them on board but the armed women are unmoved. A group of well-to-do, serious faced travellers wait, furtively glancing at the distance, inching closer to the water. Further gunfire sounds in the distance - it is drawing closer. Panic flares on the faces of waiting passengers. Gwendoline leaves the group and advances toward Rohan, going to support him around his waist.

"Hello, good timing. Nimh - I'm Gwen. You won't regret coming with us."
"There was an attack on my Unit-"
Gwendoline extends a card. Nimh looks at it. Gwendoline is clearly the bearer of an elite position, the card is genuine.

"I don't know who to tell..."
Gwendoline reads Nimh's ashen face.
"We can radio back from the boat. This is the last one. Let's

get your stuff, now." Despite the chaos, Nimh is standing there, uncertain.

"You're a 1%er. The Unit won't tell you this, but you have earned privilege. You can help your father."

"They did tell me... I haven't earned it yet, the centre is in Glasgow..."

"We can manage the disease in Iceland. You have a duty to ensure the safe passage of a Founder over serving with an attack unit. I will sign off on that." A crush toward the dock, off Nimh's face, the mask of duty gone.

Grey clouds overhead as Nimh almost asleep on Rohan's lap. People have made themselves comfortable in the cabin for the long journey ahead, the atmosphere is convivial but contained. Some of the Passengers hold heavy discussions, others confer with tablets and note-papers. It is an elite crowd. Gwendoline nurses a cup of tea, they sit quietly.

"Are your legs hurting?"

"It's worth the pain."

"I can shift her here if you like."

Rohan shakes his head, stroking Nimh's hair where the harbour's sea has not washed off the caked blood.

"She slept in our bed until she was nearly four. I was doing shift work so it was really just Marian and her. Then one day, Marian decided - intuited - the little one needed her own space. So in the space of a couple of days she gave up her office, the only space in our tiny flat for her illustrations and ideas... and turned it into the most beautiful room. The most exquisite magical garden, painted by hand. The first night it was ready, as soon as Nimh's pajamas were on she dutifully put herself to sleep in her new bed, without a backwards glance. Marian cried herself to sleep."

Gwendoline smiles. The waves beat against the boat outside, the grey clouds hover above them.
"Change can be very painful."
"She said... you see, it was just us three then. New town, no family. No sitters or grandparents to help. Just us, every second, every day. Marian took the brunt of it. She said that first night... that the past three years had been...Like swimming in the sea on a summer's day, only coming to the surface to take in gulps of air. She could hear the chatter and laughter of people sunning themselves on the beach, umbrellas up, picnics out, swimmers splashing... but she was underwater, aware of everything, trying to appreciate it but seeing through the sting of salt water, hearing through the blur. Submerged. Then, when Nimh got a little older, finally she was above water, seeing the sunshine, enjoying the swim. And then, on that one night, all tucked up in her new bed, suddenly the beach was empty and she was sitting there utterly alone. The sun shining in the deafening quiet."

Gwendoline listens.

"Of course, I thought it was a bit over the top at the time. (looks down at Nimh) Not anymore."

The boat churns on through the water, the waves turning black.

White crests flash in the light coming off the boat's hull. The waves are pitch black, a wall of water menacing under the moonlight. Nimh sits on a bench, knees under her chin, rocked within the confines of its metals bars, staring at the sky. Intermittent glimpses of the stars above, breaking through cloud cover.

Gwendoline appears at the door, a woolen blanket and some aspirin in hand. She walks up to Nimh, looks up at the same stars.

"The Vikings sailed these seas in an open boat... All the way from Norway. A thousand years ago."
Nimh listens.
"Raping and pillaging as they went?"

"Sometimes. But they were also great tradespeople, artisans, poets. And they established one of the oldest democracies. In Iceland."
"So they conquered it?" Gwendoline sits down next to Nimh.

"Settled. No humans to conquer, just an empty, untamed land of Fire and Ice." "I always thought there were Inuits... Isn't Bjork Icelandic?"
Gwendoline laughs.
"No. She's Viking Icelandic, through and through."

They sit in silence.
"This headache is agonising."
"Ah, I brought these for you."

She passes the aspirin and water. Nimh takes them. "How hard did you fall? Do you remember anything?"

"I didn't fall. I was thrown. I think I sort of woke up, it was probably just seconds. "I can't talk about it. I should check on Dad."

"He's sleeping. He's had something to ease the pain."

"How many more days until we get there?"

"I don't know. Probably about five."

Nimh sighs.

"When we get there... I'm going to do the best I can-"

"Thanks."

"But, I think he is more advanced than he's letting on. I haven't been able to see his arms at all. The treatment gets less and less effective as the symptoms advance."

A long silence fills the space.

"How long as he worn his watch in his shirt pocket?"

Nimh looks pained.

"I don't know. Not long. There are plenty of men onboard - the one with the beard –" "Dr Hessel."

"- he was shaking and then pulled a bottle out of his pocket and was fine fives minutes later."

"He's diabetic."

"Bullshit. He's got it. Why can't we borrow some stuff to give to Dad and get more when we land?"

"It doesn't work like that Nimh."

"Why?"

"Dr Hessel has a Nobel Peace Prize. (off Nimh's growing anger) Nobody knows what supplies the Island will still have."

"You said there weren't any gangs."

"There weren't, but there's been a communication issue."

"Like what?"

"No one's been in contact for two weeks."

A beloved face is drawn, brow dotted with perspiration again.

I got to change the world.

Have some water.

I got to change the world.

He smiles, that serious, gentle smile.

I get to leave the world a better place. Because I left you in it.

That's a hell of a thing to live up to Daddy.
Falling asleep on those broad shoulders, her eyes scrunched tightly.

The water is calm, a band of pink clouds streaks the lemon yellow horizon. Land is in sight.

Nimh stares.
"I'm not burying him at sea."
Gwendoline stands back, eyes pink, head bowed.
"I know."
Two letters in Nimh's hand.
"He wants to be taken to Pingvellir. I don't even know what

that is." "It's a place."
She moves to the bench, lowers herself in deference.

"It was once the seat of an extraordinary civilization... until a thousand years ago Icelandic settlers surrendered their beliefs to Christian invaders in order to prevent war. The chief law-speaker, a pagan, looking for compromise with the incoming Christians, threw the icons of their Gods into the water as a gesture of contrition. Just tossed them in, Thor's Hammer, Odin's Eye... like they were trinkets. The Old Gods thrown away like confetti. Overturning centuries of culture... and ushering in the age of men. I think he wanted to be there when the balance is restored. For you."

"Who cares about symbolism now? It's fucking ridiculous. We should have chanced it and gone to Glasgow. I could have gotten him treatment there."

Gwendoline straightens herself, takes a moment and then draws closer to Nimh.

"There was never any treatment in Iceland Nimh. All he wanted was to get you to safety. That would be his panacea, his miracle."

A sombre face with huge glistening eyes. Knuckles raw. A bad habit, corrected. The stiff starched Nuns of the Order of Friendship alive when the cane draws blood.

A little girl dreams. Under her breath she mouth the mantra, Mummy and Daddy will come, Mummy and Daddy will come.

Parched mouth, blood residue, hair matted like a feral thing from the wilds of Sherwood.

A cool hand and a warm cup of tea. The wild one drinks. Sweet civilizing nectar. Nimh looks deeply at this soft and strange outsider.
"I still don't understand what you get out of it."
Gwendoline speaks softly.

"The future is compassion."

CODA

A cold crisp night, Þingvellir National Park, Iceland. A huge valley with cascading waterfalls and black rock cliffs; the sun high in the sky at midnight. Purple and blue clouds streak the horizon. Thousands of women and dozens of men converge upon the rocky outcrop on foot, horseback, by car. bringing hope, bringing children, bringing themselves. A tall, willowy figure stands at the head of a waterfall in a crescent of other women. It is Gwendoline. She watches as the people gather. From behind, a young face appears beside her. Battered watch on a chain around her neck. Tranquil, confident with a keen intelligence and maturity in her eyes. Nimh.

ABOUT THE AUTHOR

Little is known about the author.

www.ingramcontent.com/pod-product-compliance
Lightning Source LLC
Chambersburg PA
CBHW020310150626
46552CB00022B/2552